CHAME[illegible]ON

Beda Higgins

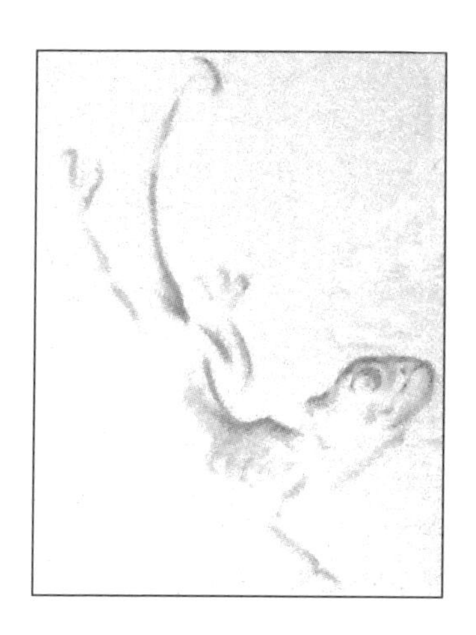

Acknowledgements

Thanks to Peter Mortimer, for publishing me and for being
an all-round good human being. Thanks to Irmgarde Horsley for proof reading most of the stories, and Joseph Higgins for proof reading. Thanks to Tom Higgins for the front cover of *Chameleon*, and Rachel Higgins for comfort breaks. Thanks to Bernard Higgins for topping my wine glass up, it's always half full. Thanks to the fabulous five; Ann, Cath, Meg, Maura and Angie for being fabulous, and thanks to my womb buddy Martin, we go back a long way. A very big thanks to New Writing North who have supported me at all stages of my writing.

Cinderella was a commissioned story for short story day Dec 21st 2010, www.nationalshortstoryday.co.uk

Bird flu was first published in a Biscuit anthology "on new street" 2006

Beda Higgins writes poetry and prose and is published in various anthologies and collections. In 2004 she received a Northern Promise Award for her first novel, and her second novel was one of five short-listed in the Lit Idol 2004 competition. In 2010 she received a Time to Write Award to complete her third novel. She works part-time as a Practice Nurse and has received two Queen's Nursing Institute Awards to fund studies to consider writing as a therapeutic tool. She lives in Newcastle upon Tyne and is married with three children.

This is Beda Higgins' debut collection of short stories.

For my family with love.

Contents

9 Haunted

17 The Quiet man

25 True Love

33 Poor Clare

41 Dark Side of the Hill

53 Footsteps

61 The Far Room

69 Cuckold

75 Festive Greetings

83 Bird Flu

91 Cinderella

101 Idle Hands

HAUNTED

THE HOUSE NEXT TO OUR SCHOOL IS HAUNTED, EVERYONE knows. It stands alone beyond the creepy pond where a girl once fell in and drowned. She was dragged under by the pond's tentacles, it wanted her for its own dark greed. She's the one that haunts the house, she's still under the water, trying to get back and looking for her revenge. She cries; I've heard her wailing through the trees, hoping someone will pull her out. Some people say she has a baby with her, a baby she had through a forbidden love. It's not allowed to go to the haunted house. In assembly Mrs Parker said it was dangerous, so everyone goes. You can get there by squeezing in-between thick bushes at the bottom of the playing field. We dare each other, except Misha who's in a wheelchair and it's not worth the bother.

The pond is green; you can smell the evil slime in it. There are weeping willow trees round it that cry dry tears. The pond is dark and shadowy, trying to hide the wicked secret, so many shades of green it can confuse you. You can see how easily the girl got muddled and tried to get back to the house. She must've panicked and fallen, her screams swallowed in thick green milkshake.

There are two old people who live in the house who never die. They are both about a hundred and fifty years old, they move like dead people do, everyday another little death shuffle. They never leave the house and no one calls round. They are the girl's parents. It's their fault she died. They found out she was having a baby and went crazy shouting and screaming at her. They threatened to drown the baby or cut its throat rather than bring shame on the family. She ran away terrified, blinded by fear, running wildly. They told everyone she'd gone away, was working abroad, but she's there, I've seen her. Her hair's tangled up in plant tendrils, she has her eyes open, and if you stand long enough you can see her wave her arms begging. Her face changes through the year but even in summer I can see she's frozen in fear, she didn't want to die. If she came nearer to the surface I would try and pull her out, but she stays deep. Some people in my class have never seen her, never seen her beautiful dark eyes. It's a gift to be able to see her like I can.

I tell Mum about the haunted house. She says "nonsense, there's no such thing as ghosts." Then she asks "what mark did you get for your Maths homework?"

I wonder why adults always try to hide the truth from kids. I watch Mum while she's cooking, she has a new wrinkle on her nose and veins on her legs. When she coughs it sounds like a crisp packet being scrunched up. I can see she's getting older. I wonder how near she is to dying.

Me and my best friend Gemma go to the pond nearly every day in the summer term. We dare each other through the bushes. I'm much braver than Gemma, but I always pretend to be scared because it's fun. Once we get through the bushes it's a different dark world, sunlight can't get in.

'Can you feel the cold chill of death?'

'Yeah I always can.'

'And the smell of rotting flesh?'

'Yuk'

'And shhhhh, listen, can you hear her crying?'

'It's so sad isn't it?'

We make up stories about the beautiful young woman and her baby. We fall a bit in love with her and honour her death by cutting our fingers to mingle our blood. It hurts, but we're in this together now, 'til death do us part.

Lily joins our class half-way through year five. She's very pretty and her Dad is a doctor. They move into the big house on the hill. Everyone wants to be her friend except me. I don't like her because Mrs James asks Gemma to show her round and to look after her on her first day. Gemma links Lily's arm in a handbag kind of way, like they're old friends. They laugh and joke straight away as if they've always been at school together. I'm outside their giggles, they're in an invisible bubble I can't pop. I pretend not to care and sit next to Stacy in class to show Gemma I'm angry with her, but she doesn't seem to notice. She pulls her chair up next to Lily and shows her how to do cat's cradle which any idiot can do. Lily might be pretty but she must be stupid.

Stacy smiles and says she'll be my friend. I try to smile back but she smells of vegetable soup.

Gemma and Lily sit together in all our classes, at lunch-time they walk round the playground like Siamese twins. After school they walk home glued together even though it's out of Gemma's way to go past Lily's house. I pretend I don't care and join in the big skipping rope game in the playground. We take turns jumping in and out, but it's boring, I wish I was still Gemma's best friend. I have a funny feeling in my tummy as if it's got a food mixer inside and my eyes are stinging. Me and Gemma have been best friends for ever, I can't believe she's being so mean.

Lily invites Gemma to a sleepover at the weekend. I watch Lily flick back her stupid long blonde hair and blink her big blue eyes and feel red and angry.

On Saturday I wake early and I want to do something; anything. I feel cross and want to hit something or someone hard. I couldn't sleep thinking about them together. I imagined them laughing and getting into their pyjamas, having a mid-night feast. I bet the house is lovely inside. I bet her room is pink and everything matches, pillowcases and duvets, not all mixed up like at our house. I bet she has a fancy bathroom with a shower and one of those things to wash your bum in. Her Mum will be pretty and her Dad handsome; he'll call her darling a lot, and say how kind Gemma's been helping her to settle in, and they'll offer Gemma more chocolate fudge cake, because I bet that's what they have for pudding there, and I bet they have serviettes.

I dare myself to go to the pond at the haunted house on my own. I've never done this before but I want to let evil soak into me, I want to be bad. There's no one around. It's weird being in the empty school playground, I can hear my heart going faster and faster. I creep through the bushes and hold onto the weeping willows while my feet slip and slide. I go as near to the pond as possible. I wish the girl under the water would reach out one of her white arms and grasp her long fingers round my ankle; then I could scream and scream, and kick out hard.

I have a feeling she knows I'm here. I hold my breath waiting, but the pea soup surface stays calm. Some of the branches are stronger than others, I grab hold of one and then carefully balancing my feet, I snap the next one in two. I push it back together so you can't tell, but I know which one it is. I stay a long time edging round the pond, I want something to happen. Little darts of sunlight makes patterns on the ground and the wind's whispering. I can feel the ghost, she's next to me, it's not the wind; it's her.

When I get home Mum goes nuts. 'What were you thinking of going off on your own without telling me?' And 'Where have you been? Your trainers are filthy, take them off you've got mud on the carpet.' She goes to the cleaning cupboard to get Mr Muscle or something that'll get marks out of the carpet. Sometimes all she's bothered about is how clean the house is. I feel like rubbing dirt and muck all over the place, smearing it on the walls to really give her something to scrub. I bet Lily's Mum has a cleaner. My Mum would be beautiful too if all she had to do all day was sit on a settee and paint her nails, or to tell the cleaner what to dust, but my Mum has to work. She also looks after

Grandma who lives near us but can't get out so Mum does all her shopping. Dad is meant to have me and my brother at weekends so Mum can have a rest but he usually doesn't. She has new wrinkles on her nose because she has to work so hard, and is a bit fat because she works in Asda and can pick up the out of date stuff really cheap, but it has to be eaten straight away. I know she would be beautiful if things were different, if she had a nice husband who gave her presents and took her out.

I hate Mrs James for asking Gemma to look after Lily, I would've done it better. If I'd have gone to Lily's house for tea I would say *please* and *thank you*, and I'd make them my chocolate brownies which are scrummy. They would love me to come again, and I'd hear them say to Lily *you're so lucky to have a lovely friend like Kirsty*.

I sit in my bedroom at my dressing table. I feel full up with green stuff from the pond, it's there making me feel sick. I can't stop thinking of Lily and Gemma and I want to hurt them both. I turn my jewellery box ballerina on and watch it go round and round, it makes a tinkling tune. I watch the girl spin slowly, she is slim and has long blonde hair. She reminds me of Lily. I put my hand round the ballerina and bend the figure over, pushing hard as I can until it snaps. I throw her out the window, it makes me feel better.

On Monday I go straight up to them. 'Have you showed Lily the pond and garden?'

'No.'

'Well some friend you are.'

'What garden?' asks Lily in her stupid posh voice.

'Over there behind the bushes at the bottom of the playing field there's a haunted house, everyone knows about the haunted house.'

Lily grabs Gemma's arm, 'Oh let's go, I love ghosty things.'

Gemma shrugs and won't look at me, 'it's nothing really.'

I sniff, 'maybe Gemma's scared of the house and that's why she's never taken you. I'll take you this lunch-time if you want.'

'Great, thanks,' says Lily who I think wears perfume.

Lily races out of class at lunch and up to me, her eyes are shiny. 'Shall we go?'

'Come on then.'

Gemma hangs back behind her, she knows I'm mad at her, I will never forgive her.

I lead Lily through the thickest bit of the hedge so she'll get scratched and cut. I let the branches flick back and don't warn her where the sharp ones are. She whimpers quite a lot and says 'ouch' but sticks with me.

Gemma fusses behind, 'Oh Lily are you okay?' and 'there's an easier way through.'

It's too late for that. I wallop down the slope to the pond as fast as I can holding onto the willow trees hoping she'll come skidding down after me and fall in. She keeps close behind and treads carefully making sure she doesn't slip in the mud.

The surface of the pond is shimmering with a kaleidoscope of green patterning. It's a hot day and the air feels damp and clammy, flies are hovering everywhere, I can taste the darkness.

'Where does the ghost live?' Lily asks. I can hear her breathing fast.

'Under the water, can't you see her?' I ask as if she's stupid.

'You're too near,' Gemma whines.

She's pathetic, I know she's never seen the girl under the water like I do, she just says she does.

'You have to come nearer,' I tell Lily ignoring Gemma.

Gemma stays at the top of the bank, holding onto a branch.

I edge forward and forward. The ground's muddy, I can see my footprint from Saturday; I know the branches to trust and the broken one. My ankles are wet I'm so close to the edge, I shout over my shoulder, 'hold onto the branches like I'm doing.'

She reaches up and teeters after me. I can hear Gemma meowing like a cat, 'no, you're too near, you'll fall in.'

Lily isn't as tall as me so has to really stretch to hang on. I say to her, 'there, over there, can you see her?' I let go with one hand and point. 'Look she's got her eyes wide open near the surface, they're big and brown, she's pleading.'

'I still can't see her.' Lily's on tippy toes now, leaning forward and forward.

I say 'grab this branch, you'll be able to see her if you get just an inch closer.'

I watch her stretch her arm to reach the broken branch, her fingers are a starfish. I say 'go on', wishing her to pull the broken one and I'll hear her scream before she falls.

I have my eyes on Lily so I don't see the girl in the pond drifting towards me. She comes up to the surface, her long white arm reaches out like a swan's neck from under the water, she slides gracefully without a sound and grabs me. My branch snaps, I fall smack into her green mirror smashing it to a million sharp pieces of death.

I kick and flail and try to get my head above the water but she drags me further down and down into her empty silence. I hear distant screaming and shouting but sink further, she pulls and tugs me under, desperate not to be alone anymore. She wants me forever. Her long arms fold round me hugging closer, she wants me to be her lost baby.

Something tugs me hard the other way, it pulls and pulls, I'm being torn in two, dragged up towards the surface, away from her. She tries to tighten her grip but the slippery slime means her fingers can't hold on; I slip away from her grasp, I'm reeled upwards. The surface of the pond comes nearer, I see light; I break through the water and gasp.

Someone heaves me over to the muddy bank. I lie coughing while they wallop my back and I spit all the gunk out. It's very bright and noisy and then it's dark and silent again.

I wake up in an ambulance. I hear the siren wailing outside.

The ambulance man says, 'it's a miracle you're still alive. Your pretty little blonde friend will get a prize for being brave going in after you like that.'

I close my eyes.

At the hospital they wheel me down a corridor on a trolley and take me behind a curtain. A doctor with a spotty tie and lots of hair gel checks me over. He makes me count to ten and then asks me to count backwards. I have to follow his finger while he traces it in the air. Then I have to say some nursery rhymes. He ruffles my hair, 'you'll be okay. You've got a plucky friend there who saved you.'

I don't smile at him.

He shuts the curtains. I hear him talking with the nurse outside. 'Strange Kid; very solemn.'

'Yeah, doesn't she have amazing eyes?'

'I know, dark, deep pools you could sink into.'

I smile her knowing death smile. I see the world through her eyes now; we know it's full of evil.

The Quiet Man

Jane's alarm jerked Steve awake. It clicked into *Galaxy FM*, rapping like a woodpecker. He put the pillow over his head but could still hear Jane singing in the shower karaoke style. There was no chance of getting back to sleep, the morning traffic was building up, he could hear the blaring, hooting, revving engines. He hated the flat, hated the city, hated his new life.

Steve dragged himself groggily downstairs. She was chomping cornflakes, her lower jaw made circular horse-like movements 'Morning Sweetie-pie' she sang with her mouth still full

They'd been married six months, her third time round, his first. He'd been a confirmed bachelor and had been having his usual quiet Friday evening drink after work when she flounced into the Fox and Grapes, accidentally spilling his drink. Before he knew it, she'd bought him another, pulled up a stool and cast her net over him; reeling him in over the next six months. He can't remember asking her to marry him, she'd whisked him up in a frothy romance, confusing his shyness, 'do you love me?' she'd asked batting her eyelids. He was putty in her well manicured hands. Suddenly arrangements were being made; bridesmaids, best man, whether to have chicken or beef. He preferred beef, but said chicken to please her. He buttered his toast wearily, six months seemed a lifetime ago She was dressing for yet another interview, she breathed in, 'zip me up will you.' She was a serial quitter of jobs, there was always something that wasn't right, someone making her life *impossible*. She was dressed in black and white, sharp and snappy, too short, too tightShe twirled in the mirror, 'proper little magpie aren't I?'

Steve thought about that as she clattered out on her high stilettos, she'd stolen every minute of peace he had.

'Wish me luck.' She shoved her puckered glossy lips forward, he pecked her cheek, it was sticky and smelt of peardrops.

'Good luck.'

When the door slammed shut Steve turned the radio off, and the TV. He sat in the armchair for a minute or two, savouring the silence, the comforting tick tock of his Mother's clock on the mantelpiece. He sighed wearily and got up to straighten his tie in the mirror. He slipped his jacket on ignoring the bottle of zingy fresh aftershave she was always trying to spray him with. Steve was a carpet fitter for the local department store. They gave him the names and addresses; he measured the areas to be carpeted in silence and later sent an estimate out. He worked alone, didn't have to get involved in sales pitch and was efficient.

Jane drove CD on full blast. She wanted this job, she hummed and rapped her fingers on the wheel. At the Bluehouse roundabout she glanced left. Jane's mouth dropped wide. A woman in the adjacent car was slumped against the window, her skin grey, mouth open, eyes shut; dead. Definitely dead. Jane stared gobsmacked, a body in the car next to her, her throat tightened, heart pounding. The driver, a ferrety man moved into gear, drove forward and turned left. Jane craned watching where it went, first left straight after the roundabout. The car behind Jane blared, she had to move. She shifted gear, head buzzing. She prioritised, interview first, police later, after all the woman was already dead.

She thought the interview went well but apparently it hadn't. '*I know this is disappointing news but it was a very competitive field. We'll keep you on our list if any more vacancies come up…*'

Jane drove back home slowly at a loss. It wasn't like her, her bubble popped. She turned the CD off. At the Bluehouse roundabout she perked up, the thought of seeing the dead woman seemed to cheer her up, gave her a focus, it wasn't every day you witnessed a murder. Instead of going home she pulled into the left lane and turned left again down the street where she'd seen the car carrying the dead body go. She felt a flutter of excitement, furtively crawling the street like a detective. She imagined telling the police, she might get in the local paper, *heroine solves murder case single handedly*. It might even get into the national news.

She spotted the tatty blue escort parked halfway down the street. She parked opposite keeping the engine going. The house was a dump. Net curtains half hung, peeling paint, overgrown garden, broken pots, a window upstairs cracked and fixed with plywood. She stared chewing her nails; the house looked evil.

Over tea she told Steve.

'Pardon?' He blinked incredulously.

'I saw a dead woman on the way to my interview which by the way I turned down,' she shrugged, 'it wasn't what I wanted.'

'What d'you mean you saw a dead body?'

'She was in a car slumped in the passenger seat.'

'She was probably sleeping.'

'She was not sleeping, she was dead.'

Steve had learnt sadly, over the few months of marriage that she made things up. She embellished reality until the distinction between truth and fantasy blurred to paint her into the centre of whatever story.

'I'm going to report the incident to the police tomorrow. I've actually done all the work for them. I know where the murderer lives. Do you know I might look into a job in the police force.'

'You saw a car for a second or two at a roundabout, and a woman looked dead? They'll think you're crazy if you go to the police station with that story.'

'I'm absolutely certain she was dead.'

'They'll charge you for wasting police time.'

'Her skin was green,' she leaned across the table, her eyes wide, 'she was probably crawling with maggots inside.'

'Maybe she had car sickness?'

Jane tutted, threw her serviette down and stood up. She banged and crashed in the kitchen and spent the rest of the evening with a bottle of wine, phoning various friends, shrieking down the phone. Steve yearned for a quiet corner he could curl up in and read his book, but her voice bounced into every room. He thought back to his before life, when he lived alone in a small semi detached bungalow on a quiet estate outside the city. A pain gnawed in the pit of his belly, he felt it often; homesickness.

Jane lay awake that night. She hadn't liked Steve's tone of voice with her, it was out of character and he'd sewn seeds of doubt. Maybe the woman wasn't dead, maybe she was ill, having chemotherapy, that's why she looked so awful. She tossed and turned mulling it over, she needed to clarify the situation. She'd go round to the house, if she saw her alive, good and well she'd forget the whole thing. If the nasty man behaved oddly, maybe even dangerously, she'd have solved a murder. She was buoyed by the thought of stalking a killer, and turned over pulling the quilt one more time before sleeping soundly.

She woke feeling all the better for having a plan of action. She flicked the music on extra loud singing along. Steve groaned from under the duvet, he'd hardly had any sleep with all her rolling about, he didn't think he could stick it much longer.

Jane drove slowly and drew up outside the run-down house. The blue death car was there. She checked her lipstick in the mirror and got out, holding her head high; she had a job to do. She rang the doorbell and waited on the doorstep, it smelt of cat's pee. After a few minutes she realised the bell wasn't working and rapped on the door, her knuckles hurt. A man answered, scruffy, about forty, unshaven, mullet haircut, unwashed.

'Yeah?'

The carpets she could see behind him were threadbare, a smell of grease and something sharper, a dead body?

She cleared her voice, 'I'm doing a survey on beauty products, is your wife in?'

'I don't have a wife.'

'Your partner or any female resident who lives here?'

'I live alone, so you're wasting your time.' He narrowed his sharp eyes.

She felt a shiver of fear and stepped away. 'Oh right, well sorry for disturbing you.'

He slammed the door shut.

Jane drove away shakily, a flutter in her belly. She was on her way to the police station with her valuable information when she wondered should she delve a little more. She knew she was a natural for the job, she could get some more evidence, maybe even find the body. She'd go early tomorrow morning; he looked the sort to stay in bed late. She'd check the back garden for fresh digging, if anyone asked questions she'd say she lost a ring yesterday while conducting her questionnaire. She felt a thrill jangle down her spine, here she was dabbling into the darker side of life, who'd have thought.

She was high as a kite until Steve lumbered home and dampened her spirits. His disapproval hung over their plate scraping, fork shovelling, mug slurping tea. She blurted it out trying to sound nonchalant, 'I was at a loose end today so I popped down Ethel Street and knocked on the door of the dead woman.' She gushed, she didn't want him interrupting and spoiling it. 'A sinister character opened the door, he had murderer written all over his face. I had to think on my feet and asked him could I speak to the lady of the house, said I was doing a survey on cosmetics.'

Steve's eyes were growing wider and wider, bulging in disbelief, 'please tell me you are joking.'

'Course I'm not, I'll hand the case over to the police tomorrow. I'll get an application form to join up while I'm there.'

'You're living in cloud cuckoo land.'

'I beg your pardon?' Jane's cheeks flushed.

'You're a living lie. You exist in a pretend world where you are the most important person, the world revolving around you; ME ME ME that's all that matters.'

Jane stood aghast, what had happened to mealy mouthed Steve who wouldn't say boo to a goose. For once in her life she was speechless.

Steve pushed himself away from the table, 'have a nice day chasing fantasies, some of us have a mortgage to pay. Maybe you should go to the police, with a bit of luck they'll lock you up and I'll get a bit of peace and quiet at last.'

Jane stared at the slammed door for quite some time.

The following evening Steve drove wearily back home. His job covered the whole county, sometimes he did up to a hundred miles a day; he'd covered plenty that day. He loosened his tie while driving and had radio four on low, unobtrusive, calming voices dipping and ebbing. The news was bad as usual, another bomb in Afghanistan, an oil slick off Ireland, people randomly stabbed, strangled or shot, a drought in India. He turned the radio off and listened to his thoughts instead.

Steve opened the flat door slowly, he was tired, it had been a long day. He dropped his suitcase on the floor exhausted. The house was quiet, he could hear the clock tick, it was strange; she always left the TV on. He made a cup of tea, and half heartedly grazed a pizza he found in the fridge. Ten minutes later the doorbell rang, a shadowy figure stood behind the frosted door. He opened it, the young spotty officer and policewoman looked sad, 'we're sorry to have to inform you…'

Steve went to pieces. When he could speak coherently he answered their questions between gulps and sighs.

'Have you any idea who might've done this?'

Steve waved his head side to side, 'there was a man, I'm not sure if this is relevant…'

'Please go on, anything might be helpful.'

'Jane was convinced a man had killed a woman.' He sniffed, 'she said she'd seen the woman's dead body in his car. I know she'd gone to find where he lived.' He dropped his head into his hand. 'I didn't take her seriously, I wish I'd listened, she might not be…' he sobbed again.

They brought him water and let him compose himself.

'She said she'd spoken to him, she was shaky, I'm not sure if he'd threatened her. Like I say, I thought she was letting her imagination get the better of her.' He bit his lip, biting back the tears.

They gave more water, more back patting sympathy.

'She was going to report it all to the police today. Jane wanted to be as helpful as she could be, she was trying to get evidence, it was important to her that the police believed her, she was thinking of applying to join the force.'

They nodded their heads encouragingly. Steve went on 'Christ why didn't I listen to her.' He clutched his head sobbing.

'Can you tell us this man's address?' they asked gently.

'I know it's somewhere off the Bluehouse roundabout, and he drives an old blue Escort.'

'We'll do everything we can to catch this brutal killer.'

'Can you tell me how she died?' he asked shakily.

'Strangled. She was found in a lay-by, there's no evidence of any other assault, if that's of any comfort.'

They left him about half an hour later; a broken man.

He stood in the dark and watched their tail lights disappear into the night. He took the phone off the hook, he didn't want to talk to anyone. He unplugged the TV, radio and DVD.

He closed the windows muffling the traffic outside. He disconnected the doorbell.

He stepped out into their small back yard. It was the quietest spot, not overlooked with only the faintest hum of cars and bird calls in a distant sky. He sat on the bench for hours undisturbed, soaking in the silence and watched the sky melt into darker hues, until it was the same shade of purple her face had been.

True Love

It was my first summer job and I nearly got the sack the first week for spreading the egg mayonnaise too thick. Julie the Manageress with plucked eyebrows and a leopard skin skirt shooed me into the kitchen, showing me step by step how to do them properly, I had to mix in more margarine and mayonnaise with the eggs.

'You should get eight rounds to two eggs, they just want something to sop up their tea.'

So I got the knack of spreading little yellow lumps thinly across white squares. When it looked like porridge, it was perfect. Once I'd finished the sandwiches, cut them into triangles and covered with cling film, I was allowed in to watch the show.

Blackpool had hundreds of shows in the summer, this one was touted as "different" a Tyrolean show. Grown men in leather shorts and women in twirly skirts with yellow plaits, warbled and danced to the dulcet tones of Reg on the organ. Reg could've been eighty, but with his jet black toupee and red waistcoat he was a grown-up Pinnochio. The performers had all had glory days; The Winter Gardens, the Piers, and the Palladium. Each tale of fame came with curled photos tucked in pockets and wallets. Now, well past their sell by dates, they were ripe for the Tyrolean show.

The show opened with George and Giselle's magic tricks. They were slick and quick. How did he know that was the right card? And how did he chop her in two? That was the magic, y'd never know.

Bill was next, the yodeling comic. He'd have them in tucks with his innuendo and muck. Nearly all the audience came on coaches, if it was a Yorkshire crowd he'd call the Lancashire folk Dipsticks, and if it was a Lancashire crowd, he'd call the Yorkshires tight fisted. They loved that, ethnic cleansing was always popular.

There'd be a bit of singing then, with Reg plonking his keys. Stuff like *Daisy, Daisy, give me your answer do…* and *It's a long way to Tipperary, it's a long way to go….* Glaswegians were the best, tanked up to the eyeballs the whole audience would sway; a sea of red faced ginger nuts linking sunburnt sweaty arms, chafing hot thighs, bobbing on the tide. When they got to the *I'm half crazy all for the love of you* I'd see the oldies look at each other and wipe a tear away. Next Doreen would come on and do a solo. She had a lovely voice, a dead ringer for Shirley Bassey. When the curtain came down for the interval, it was all ravings at the butty bar. 'In't it a smashing show.'

The curtain went up for the second half and Bill was back on with his smut and grease. Sometimes he'd pick on someone in the audience, make a right fool of them, but they never seemed to mind, shining fat faced. He knew the ones who'd be up for it. Mother-in law jokes, and his bums and tits always went down a treat.

At the end of the week I could see the show was naff except for the bit with Jim and Davey. I could watch that performance again and again. I know it sounds corny, but it was dead romantic. Jim was about sixty and did a turn with his exotic bird called Davey, it was the climax of the show. Davey sat in Jim's pocket until Jim whistled a soulful lullaby, at which point Davey poked his little head out. Jim, dewy eyed would whisper, stroking the dappled head, calming his quivering chest. He whispered a language only for themselves and Davey would fly gently out of his pocket trilling to his song. Two kindred spirits entwined in the air, Jim whistled and Davey warbled to his tune. As he flew round the theatre, you could shut your eyes and escape on those tiny fluttering wings. The song ended on a quivering note of pure joy. The bird soared and dived down back into Jim's chest pocket, lying next to his heart where he belonged. They usually had at least two encores. It was dreamy, the invisible thread between them.

At the end of the evening Jim'd nod his head and smile, 'I'll see you all tomorrow then.' He was like that, a proper gentleman. Popping his hat on, he'd peep in at Davey snuggled in his pocket, and off they'd go. He never stayed for a drink, he was happy enough just himself and Davey.

The rest of us would lounge round the bar. I loved the tired smokiness. The laziness, lolling over chairs, arms resting on each other's shoulders, old jokes again and again. Me and Mark became mascots of the show. He'd asked me out on the first night of working there, he helped behind the bar, even though he was under age. The likes of Joan and Giselle thought we were sweet. Mark'd sit looking doe-eyed stroking my arm, until he could walk me to the bus stop.

'Ahhh aren't they a picture, give 'em another drink there Steve, Eh d'y' remember being young and in love?'

I didn't know what love was, but this was okay. I'd please them feeling tiddly on my Babychams and squeeze Mark's hand. Joan'd peel her false eyelashes off and take the falsies out of her Tyrolean teasy blouse which collapsed like popped bubblegum. George pulled off his wig and wiped his bald bonce, it was shiny and pink. They'd reminisce and laugh loud. The takings were good, Julie let everyone have a round of drinks free. It was warming up to be one of the best seasons and Julie said I could do the egg butties a bit thicker.

Mark would walk me to the bus stop. The summer sky was dark blue with diamond press studs holding the clouds together. We'd huddle in the bus shelter for a chance of touchie feelie snogging. Sometimes a car would beep and we'd snuggle deeper in the corner, it smelt of wee, but we didn't care. Mark would stand with his arms round me, looking over my shoulder so I didn't miss the bus, it was the last one. He always waited until the bus was out of sight, waving to me, looking lonely. People on the bus smiled at his little matchstick figure in the distance.

Four weeks into the job I was an old hand at it. I knew the short changers, how to look at miserable gits straight on so they didn't bother complaining about their eggless bread, and how to smile for "And keep the change love." I could make pots of tea, and slice Dundee cake at the same time as ringing up the till.

'She's a great little worker that one.'

'Yeah, she's great' mooned Mark. That night at the bus stop he said it. Squeezing my tits, breathing hot in my ear, 'I love you.' It was like in a magazine, the stars were bright and the lightest of warm breezes lifted my hair. I felt him kiss my neck, then his lips on mine for a long time, like on tele; a lover's kiss. He didn't smile, just looked seriously into my eyes, so I wanted to look away, and he said it again, 'I love you.'

I felt kind of awkward, so I said 'and I love you.'

He hugged me so long and tight I missed the bus. He walked me home and said he was glad because it meant he had more time with me. He squeezed my hand saying he was so happy, he skipped along. My feet were tired, I felt fat because I was due on, and to be honest was glad to wave him 'bye' at our garden gate, hoping my lips didn't look swollen so that I'd get ear ache from my Mum and Dad. I waved him off and felt a bit guilty to be relieved to see him go, but dead excited at the same time, this was really heavy. I wrote it in my diary as soon as I got in. "Mark and I are in love, he loves me." It was like having a hidden treasure, something mega to show off about.

I rang Jenny the next morning, 'Guess what?'

'What?'

'Go on guess'

'You've won the lottery.'

'Better than that.'

'It better had be, you've woken me up.'

'Mark says he loves me.'

'You're kidding.'

'No, last night, it was so romantic, and I love him.'

'Oh my God, are you going to do it.'

'I think we might.'

'Oh my God I can't believe you're going to do it.'

When I thought of *it*, it made me not want to think about *it*, or Mark singing to the stars. It was exciting, but I wished; I don't know what I wished, maybe that I felt like singing to the stars too.

The next week was the Glaswegian's. It couldn't get much better than this. They'd laugh at any old Land-lady joke, and sing along to Reg's wayward notes. And then it happened during Tuesday's rehearsal, the worst; the very worst. Jim found a ball of death in his pocket, Davey died next to his heart.

It hurt just to look at Jim, he was felled. I could tell he was in shock or something, he stared at the feathers, flesh and bones, cold in his cupped hands. After what seemed like forever he carried him gently out of the theatre. We left him to it, nobody said a word. As the door shut behind them, Julie said, 'rehearsals cancelled this afternoon.'

I think Jim took him down to the sea for a proper burial. When he came back we all chivvied him along, not looking at his red ringed filmy eyes. His skin was ashen, he looked crumpled up. Julie dragged him out straight away for another partner. 'After all the show must go on, y'know.'

Jim flinched.

For a week Jim's spot was filled with a few songs from George and Giselle, the audience were restless. 'Where's the bloke and his Budgie? Best bit of the show him.'

Jim was back stage teaching his new bird how to do tricks. He looked as pretty as Davey to me, but Jim was broken hearted, he kept looking at the ceiling, as if he might see Davey fly back, just a glimpse. It was all he could do to train the bird to fly round the stage. Most of us thought Jim should have compassionate leave, to get over it, but Julie was less patient. 'It was only a bleedin' bird y'know.'

That night at the bus stop Mark whispered, 'I couldn't bear to lose you.'

It worried me, because I thought I'd get over him in a week or two, and I enjoyed imagining Jenny cooing round me with, 'you'll get over him, everyone has a broken heart sometime.' I thought how strange love is, affecting people in different ways.

We were all a bit nervous for Jim on his first outing with the new bird. His whistling was wobbly and to be honest a bit flat, but the show went on. The bird took to the air as soon as Jim undid his pocket. I bet it hated it in there, holed up in a dead bird's grave. Soon the bird could-n't be arsed. It flew where it pleased, darting round the theatre, crap-ping on some of the ginger nuts, who shouted out very rude words at poor old Jim.

Jim didn't seem to be able to muster enough strength to control the bird, and slid off the stage just missing the popcorn missiles. Julie got up sharpish with, 'apologies for the technical hitch folks, and free ice creams for everyone. All we want is for you all to have a good time.'

The bird soared, dipped and dived, enjoying its new found freedom.

Jim never got to grips with another bird, never got over Davey. He officially retired, and didn't bother to have a leaving 'do'.

I don't know why, but I couldn't stop thinking about him. Eventually I visited him in his dingy flat, he didn't live far from us, and I felt sorry for him. The flat was small and shabby. The walls were yel-low, the furniture tired and brown. The floor was sticky linoleum, curl-ing at the edges. Through some dangly beads I saw Jim's bed, it was unmade, blankets in a heap. Nothing was special. The light bulbs did-n't have shades, and some artificial flowers were so faded, they were almost transparent. Everything had a twilight half-life, even his tea was weak and washy, I think he forgot to put the bag in.

We sat at his small table and had our tea. I told him how the show was going, and how we all missed him, and how the punters kept asking when would he be back. I told him Bill caught the new bird and took him to the sea front, setting him free. Jim nodded, quietly supping his tea. I said I was back at school next week, this was my last week at the show. Then he asked, 'how's Mark? I've rarely seen a lad so smitten.'

I said 'he's fine' but looked away, feeling flustered, and it was like Jim knew I was lying. So I asked Jim a question, 'how d' you know when you're in love?'

He smiled. It was the first time I'd seen him smile since Davey. 'You'll know.' And that's all he said. He patted my hand, his hands were papery and cold. They felt like dried leaves in autumn, neither alive nor dead.

I wrote in my diary that night. "Not sure that I do love Mark"

After my last night at the show, I told Mark at the bus stop. It was terrible, even though I'd timed it so there was only five minutes before the bus came, it was like hours of sniveling. 'What have I done wrong? Can't we start again? Give me another chance.'

I felt dead guilty and hopped on the bus - no looking back.

Two weeks later I saw Mark down the town with Jenny. His arm round her, she was resting her head on his shoulder, looking up at him as if they were in love. I watched them kiss, and as the bus pulled away I wondered what it'd be like to kiss Jenny, I bet she'd taste nice. I felt hot and weird. Jim was right, I wondered how old I'd be before I found a *true* love that'd really break my heart.

Poor Clare

SHE LIKES THE CONTAINMENT OF SEWING, SMALL PRECISE stitches, her back curved to the chink of light. Sometimes she pricks herself and squeezes her finger until it bleeds; to see the colour. Her nimble clever fingers sew in and out, little squares and triangles of holy bodies. She prays for all the lost souls, especially one. Often she hears the voice of a child; it's her cross to bear. She splits the difference between then and now; she had no choice, it's in the past, all she can do is pray.

Clare grew up in the west of Ireland. The business of surviving was priority, food to be put on the table, clothes to be put on their backs. Her Mammy wouldn't take a bit of charity, 'we'll manage.'

So they did. With prayers, the sun in their hair and the wind behind their backs. Mammy said they were blessed. Clare wasn't so sure, she'd never been to a party, and would've liked to have been.

Mammy relied heavily on her as the oldest. Clare helped with Shaun and Danny, and did more than her fair share of chores willingly. Clare knew there was a world outside the hay and mud, she'd seen it on the tele at Marie Rochford's house. She saw how other folk lived, it interested her. *Temptation* Mammy called it, but Clare wasn't so sure.

Clare used to go and read in the barn when she'd finished her jobs, she liked the peace and quiet away from the boys, and could read what she liked away from Mammy who was funny about books, she didn't want Clare's imagination filled with filth. Sometimes Clare took her radio with her and listened to *The Beatles*, Mammy didn't like them either.

The Burn's nephew from Dublin was staying that summer to help Paddy Burn as he'd broken his ankle, he still had an awful limp slowing him down. The nephew was seventeen. She'd heard he was handsome and sophisticated.

She saw him at Mass on Sunday and could feel his eyes burning into her back, they didn't speak but their eyes met. Later when the Sunday dishes were washed and put away, and the boys were out playing, she went to the barn as usual. It was a warm sunny day and the dappled dark of the barn perfect for resting back in the hay.

She didn't hear him coming so it gave her a fright to see his silhouette in the doorway, a black outline with the sun streaming behind him. He looked like a vision appearing before her.

She sat bolt upright and took a sharp breath.

He smiled, 'sorry I didn't mean to frighten you, I saw you come in here and I saw you at Mass and I thought I'd come and say hello.'

'Hello' she said timidly, grateful for the dark sparing her blushes.

'I'm staying at Paddy Burn's for the summer, it's a bit lonely.'

'I can imagine.'

The Burns never had children; it wasn't talked about; these things happen.

He stood, one foot to the other, she felt awkward sitting on the hay looking up at him and him looking down.

He stuck his hands in his pockets, 'well I'm sorry I disturbed you.'

'No you didn't, really, I'm only reading.'

'What're you reading?'

'Oh it's a school book, James Joyce.' She shoved it into the hay, she didn't want to admit to reading Mills and Boon.

'James Joyce, Oh God that fellah gives me nightmares, we had to do him last year.'

She smiled. 'What's your name?'

'John, I know yours is Clare.'

She was glad again for the dark, her face burned.

She looked up at him for several seconds. Then he coughed shuffling, 'well, I'll let you get on with your reading and see you again soon,' he added quickly 'I hope,' and left.

'Bye' she waved. She didn't take in one more word of her book that day. She tried to remember how he looked; so tall and handsome, he could've stepped straight out of one of her books. She thought of him while she milked the doe eyed cows, teasing the warm drops hanging to shoot milk into the bucket. She smiled, humming all evening.

He came again the next evening, Clare made sure she finished her jobs early and was in the barn most of the afternoon. She wore a red ribbon in her hair.

He smiled 'Hi' and came into the dark flopping down next to her on the hay. He picked up a blade of hay and chewed it. She watched his mouth move round and round. 'I'm seventeen' he said.

Clare said 'I know.' She smiled and he laughed. He didn't ask how old she was, she wanted him to think she was older than fourteen, she knew she looked it, she was glad he never asked and she didn't have to lie.

Later that evening Clare sat in front of her bedroom mirror. She had a blade of hay and put it in her mouth, moving it round like he did, but it didn't look the same. She looked at her eyes, he'd said they were nice, she wondered what it was about them he liked. John had said when he finished school he was going to London to live a little. She'd said she'd like to go to London one day too. She went to sleep dreaming of "living a little".

Clare went into the kitchen the next morning, she hummed and dipped her finger in the treacle tin Mammy had got out to make parkin for the lunchboxes. It was dark and sticky, that's what his voice was like, sweet. She licked her finger.

He came to the barn earlier the next day, 'have you finished all your jobs?'

'Clare nodded 'Yes.'

'Come on then, let's go for a walk.'

He held his hand out to pull her up. She grinned and nearly fell into him as he yanked her up, she touched his chest to steady herself, his eyes were very blue, she hoped he couldn't hear her heart thundering so loud to be near to him.

He took her down by the lake. Two swans glided by, barely rippling the water, their haughty necks high. 'They're beautiful aren't they?' she sighed.

He nodded and glanced at her, 'so are you.'

Flustered, Clare went slightly over on her ankle, he reached out and steadied her laughing, she held onto his arm and then he took hold of her hand. His hand was warm and dry, it was bigger than hers, his fingers wrapped round. She didn't want the walk to end or the day to end, she wanted him to keep holding her, to hear his voice and watch the muscles in his long arms move under his freckled skin. They went round the lake and back through the crackling, rustling woods. The sunlight danced between the trees, the air cool and dank.

Too soon, they were heading back to the farm. At the edge of the woods surrounded by trees he turned towards her and put his arms round her. He bent forward and she lifted her face to him. She'd never kissed before but had practiced on her hand. She liked the way his mouth moved round hers, the feel of his body, the smell of his skin and his arms round her. He smiled after the kiss, 'I'll be off then,' shoved his hands in his pockets and sauntered away.

They went in opposite directions. He called over his shoulder, 'see you tomorrow.'

She could hardly sleep, she licked her lips trying to re-capture his taste, the feel of his tongue. She wondered did her mouth feel the same as his. She looked in the mirror again, tried to see herself as he did. She stroked the hand he'd held. There was a life outside these wide spaces and cloud filled skies.

As soon as he came to the barn the next day and flopped down next to her they started kissing, the hay tickled but neither cared, all the time kissing and feeling and wanting it never to stop. They pushed closer and closer, she kept her eyes shut, wanting his mouth, his hands, wanting more, so hot she was burning up with hunger. She wouldn't let herself think about what they were doing, his hand down her jumper, up her skirt and somewhere, somehow, something that felt so good she wanted him never to stop. She whispered into his shoulder, 'we shouldn't be doing this.'

He stroked her hair, 'why not?'

She smiled and said nothing, the only reason she could think of was her Mammy would say she was a Jezabel. He nuzzled against her neck, 'I love you.'

She lifted his head cupping it in her hands. She stared into his eyes shining in the dark, and without a word bent and kissed slow and long.

They drank each other in. He kissed her breasts, kissing her belly, and on down, she breathed faster, her head moving, strange animal noises coming from inside her, *don't stop*, she wanted him never to stop. Skin on skin, breathing faster until they fell off a cliff, plummeting blind for seconds, soaring.

Clinging to him she opened her eyes, she was amazed to be still alive. She knew what had happened but didn't believe it, she can't have, she should've said, *stop, we can't, it would be wrong* but didn't; nothing in her life had ever felt so right.

She put her clothes back on in silence, the world was still turning, the sun setting; orange and crimson fingers melted at the barn door. He smiled sheepishly 'You okay?'

'Course I am,' but when she stood up her legs were shaking.

They met the next day, her heart quickening, she wanted his hands all over her, inside her again, to feel that feeling, but was cautious, she'd been scared of how she felt, and wanted to keep in control.

He fell next to her and kissed, she sucked his mouth, but after a few seconds pushed him back, 'I think we need to be more careful.'

They linked fingers and lay on the hay, talking quietly. He told her 'my little brother is coming soon to help out on uncle's farm too, it'll change everything; he's a pest.'

The brother arrived the next day. He was always hanging round, his nosy beak wherever John went. They never had the chance to be alone.

Two weeks later John came to say goodbye before he went back to Dublin. He brushed her hair back, 'I'll keep in touch. I'll never forget you.'

She squeezed his hand, 'please come back again soon.'

His poxy brother appeared at the barn and wolf whistled, they jumped apart.

The week after, Clare went back to school. It all seemed a dream or a story out of one of her books. She tried to remember exactly his face, but all she could remember in startling clarity was the kick he gave her inside.

She started getting fat through the winter, she cut her calorie intake down and went to church a lot. She lit candles at the foot of the Virgin Mary. It was a cold miserable winter, lots of layers of baggy clothes needed, everyone waddled round like sheep. She grew unnoticed, did her jobs, kept her head down, she'd always been the quiet studious sort.

The pain started on St Patrick's day, but didn't stop until St Joseph's day, March 19th. She lay in the barn alone and afraid, it was out of her hands, nature would run its course. It hurt more than when she'd had toothache, worse than when she'd broken her arm. She thought it'd never end.

She smuggled the wet creature deep in her coat, out from the barn of rusty hay into a cold shrinking evening. She walked past the humming hedges covered in mantilla cobwebs, all grieving. The frosty hills peered down at the new born shining pale.

She hoped she wouldn't burn in hell. A candle of hope snuffed out as she dropped it in a ditch, and saw it kick like a jelly fish with head and legs. An arrow of crows shot by startling her, she sobbed and left.

As the days and weeks passed by it seemed more and more that the world around her knew. Even the animals stared with knowing sharp eyes, the clouds rolled thunder, the rain pelted sinners. She was bad and wrong. She went on a pilgrimage to find out what to do, and shuffled with the cripples to beg, she was forsaken but could still pray. It was all she could do, and all she did.

Mammy stirred porridge at the stove the morning she left. She cried a lot but knew a life of devotion was something to be proud of. Clare stepped out of the house with the sun on her head and the wind behind her back, into wide white skies.

That evening in her cell Clare looked in the mirror until moonshine turned her white skin to stone. She could only pray and bandage her silence in sighs. In the morning a diamond day cut through the window, lighting a trickle down her face, she never felt warm again.

She craned out her window and saw on the ground below a shattered blue egg, dead lips, baggy veins. She knew Mother nature would never let her forget, but she was confused, tricked even; because it had felt the most instinctive natural thing in the world to be in love.

Dark Side of the Hill

WHY CAN'T WE STAY AT THE MARINA AGAIN?' GINA moaned.'It was already booked up, end of story' snapped Jeff. Mary sniffed, 'it wouldn't have been if you hadn't tried to knock them down as a *loyal customer*.' She gave Jeff yet another withering look. She'd had to plead with him to stop haggling and to get his tight-fisted hand out of his pocket, by the time he did, the Marina villa had gone. Course it had. His mean streaked stupidity still stung.

Jeff looked at his family in the airport queue. Mary had her M&S shorts and matching T-shirt on. Her orange false tan legs looked radioactive and clashed with her yellow hair. Jonny had his baseball hat on back to front, sulkily chewing gum. Gina stood lumpy and awkward in a mini-skirt, which did nothing for her legs. He sighed deeply, still smarting over the clanger with Marina, what a prick he'd been. Still, the villa they'd booked might be okay, even though it fell into *charm* category rather than their usual *luxury*.

After the inevitable hassle of collecting bags and hiring a car at Malaga airport, they drove away. Jeff hummed resting his elbow on the window, the villa they were booked into was in the vicinity of Marina so he had his fingers crossed. He knew it wouldn't top Marina, which was a palatial Andalucía house on top of the valley with spectacular views down to the sea. A sunken garden nestled round the large swimming pool, a crazy paving path led to a garden with splashes of rainbow dripping flowers and plants. Inside the villa was cool marble, the bedrooms huge, every comfort they needed, even a games room which kept the kids happy all holiday.

They were to pick the keys up from a local bar. The bar man handed them over smiling broadly. He gregariously pointed Jeff out to a man propping up the bar. They both laughed. Jeff gave a half-hearted laugh joining in; confused. He shrugged his shoulders, and squinted at the map, it looked complicated, he wanted to be in the villa before nightfall.

He handed Mary the torch. The instructions led them to a track, then a smaller track, then a dirt track. 'This can't be right,' said Mary turning the map sideways.

There was no alternative. They followed it down the mountainside, the car rocking side to side rolling in and out of pot-holes. Gina whimpered, 'I'm scared' as she stared down the sheer drop out of her window. They spiralled down and down, 'it says here after three kilometres you should come to the Abril.'

'But there's only a shed here.'

'It can't be.'

'It couldn't be.'

'Oh my God it is, look, there's a sign.'

'This is *charm*?'

Jeff's belly felt heavy. He got out of the car. 'Let's give it a chance eh? It might be fine inside.'

'What like Dr Who's Tardis?' grunted Jonny.

'Dad it's tiny,' squealed Gina.

Inside was bleak and bare. The brochures idea of *charm* was a hovel. Jeff found the light switch which threw jaundiced shadows on the walls. A huge spider scampered into a hole, Gina screamed.

'Get a grip Gina, it's only a spider.' Jeff rubbed his forehead, he was paying good money for this dump. It was getting dark, he was exhausted. 'Let's get some sleep. It might seem different in the morning.'

They reluctantly skulked off to find the bedrooms. Mary found the double room. There was no dressing table, no wardrobe, no mirror. There was nothing but a bed. She sat on it wearily and it squeaked. 'Great, all we need.'

Jonny came in, 'our rooms are tiny, the beds are little dwarf beds.'

Mary went through to them, banging her head on the low ceiling.

Gina sat dejectedly on what looked like a camp bed. 'Mum this is horrible.'

'Sssshh, I know, let's try and get some sleep and we'll have a rethink tomorrow.'

No one could wash as they couldn't get the water on. Jeff rolled over in bed and it screeched like a wildcat; sex would be tricky. A mosquito buzzed over him, he'd get some spray and kill them all tomorrow along with the holiday rep. Mary lay rigid beside him, as a creepy-crawly phobic the various scuffling scurries were her idea of hell.

They woke the following morning with an interesting collection of wheals and bumps. 'I've been bitten everywhere' wailed Gina.

'Me too' Jonny showed off a nose-sized lump on his arm.

'Come on let's get breakfast' said Jeff, 'there should be a welcome pack.'

The kitchen was dismally bare. There was a tomato, half a cucumber, a small loaf of bread, six tea bags and a plastic square of jam. The food was surrounded by ants, the place was crawling.

A voice distracted them. 'Cooee, it's Hilary, your holiday rep.'

They greeted her with four faces of abject misery.

Hilary didn't have the complexion for a holiday rep. A greasy Toby jug of a woman stood jammed in the small doorway. She held out her podgy, sweaty hand. No one reached to take it. 'Er, well pleased to meet you.'

'You won't be in a minute when I've finished with my list of complaints,' Jeff fumed. 'Can you tell me why I'm paying for this dump?'

Hilary dutifully listened. When he'd finished ranting she explained patronisingly, 'sometimes it takes a while to adjust to the rustic way of life. You come from busy homes, fully equipped with all mod cons. I'm sure by next week when you've wound down a bit you'll appreciate the simple life. I don't think there's anything deficient in the villa, it's as specified in the brochure. *Functional kitchen, homely bedrooms*, charm is basic, back to basics.'

Jeff bombarded her with complaints which Hilary politely but firmly fielded. It became apparent they hadn't a leg to stand on; he hadn't read the small print. She glanced at her watch, 'Gosh, I must dash. The emergency numbers are at the back of our brochure and on behalf of the company I'd like to wish you a super holiday.'

They lolled round their little pool. The kids couldn't have diving competitions like last year, it was too small. They jumped in for half an hour and then started rubbing their eyes, allergic to whatever was in the water. The pool patio was small and cramped, a weary brown lawn yawned round it. The sun beds uncomfortable and smelly. The view from the villa was a towering crane, and beyond they could see the Villa Marina on top of the hill.

Laughter from Marina tinkled down, splashing squeals of fun. Jeff lay pretending to read as the day dragged on. The kitchen was so basic they were reduced to sandwiches, limp and tasteless. Last year Mary had loved the kitchen at Marina, she'd imagined she was presenting a cookery programme and flounced round the well equipped huge area. Now they slumped glumly round the rickety table as wafts of delicious food floated over them from above. Mary yearned for Marina, the large barbeque space, the beautiful garden, the dripping flowers. She wanted to lie down in the big air-conditioned bedroom, they'd had the best sex there in years. There was no chance of that in this squat.

They went out to eat, it was too depressing to stay in. Gina whinged, 'everything looks horrid on me with these disgusting bites.'

'God the kids are ungrateful,' Jeff muttered to Mary.

Mary barked, 'they hate it here and so do I.'

Jeff gave a long suffering sigh, and in the silent pause, laughter and music rolled down the hill.

He decided to take them to the Bodelia Restaurant. It'd been everyone's favourite last year. This year was busier with less waiters. They glared in silence as it seemed every other table was served. The kids asked for money to go and play billiards, Jeff gave them plenty, it looked as if they were in for a long wait. Mary and Jeff sat in silence, absorbing the buzz around them, it filled their emptiness.

The kids rushed back. 'Hey guess what, we've met some really nice kids our age, and guess what?'

'What?'

They're staying at the Marina.'

Jeff said through thin lips, 'that's nice.' He didn't like them instinctively, they were staying in *their* villa.'

Gina pointed across the restaurant. A pink, shiny woman waved, she was wearing a peach dress. Mary waved back muttering, 'salmon on legs.'

They came over, 'Hi nice to meet you, so you stayed at the Marina last year? Fabulous isn't it? Where are you staying this year?'

'Oh just down the valley from you.'

'It's a dump' whined Jonny.

'Oh come on, it's not that bad.'

'No it's worse,' nodded Gina.

Jeff grinned through gritted teeth. 'Kids, never satisfied eh?'

'Steve Jackson's the name, pleased to meet you.' He thrust his hand out and shook Jeff's firmly. He was tall and lean, Jeff pulled his belly in and stood straighter. Steve went on, 'the kids seem to get on really well. Why don't you all come round for a barbeque?'

'Oh yes' Joan Jackson flapped, 'that would be super.'

'That would be nice,' said Mary, wondering what she'd done to deserve such cruel taunting.

They arranged it for the next day and waved them off.

'Dad can we stop for an ice cream?'

'No you can bloody well do without, and don't dare ever complain about this holiday in public ever again, you ungrateful wretch.'

They drove home washed in a torrent of Jeff's frustration and anger. 'I do the best I can, I work my guts out, I try to give you a good holiday and what thanks do I get? Humiliation in front of strangers, that what I get. It's not my fault this villa's not up to your standards, have you ever stopped to consider how I feel?'

They held their breath as he shifted gears, faster and faster turning sharply down the helter-skelter track to the villa. His rage roared with the engine, screeching down the spiral. The car scratched against trees, they swerved and bounced and took a 90 degree turn. Jeff screeched the brakes on.

'Oh my God,' screamed Mary, 'you're going to kill us all.'

The car skidded, lurching precariously, wavering on the track by a whisker. Gina peeked out her window through fingers to the sheer drop down below, she faintly moaned on the edge of death. The car teetered on the cliff.

'Everyone shuffle over to the right,' Jeff panted. The kids hiccoughed fear, Mary whimpered prayers. *Shuffle shuffle* they shifted across. Slowly and painstakingly Jeff managed with the handbrake and quick gear changes, with everyone leaning to the right, to get the car back on track.

There was a stunned silence while Jeff drove the last few hundred meters slower, carefully. 'Well that death trap is another fucking thing to complain about.' He wiped beads of sweat. No one uttered another word.

The next day they all spent a long time getting ready to go to the Jackson's barbeque. Everyone was in a better mood, there was something to look forward to, the drive from hell exiled to the darkest recesses of memory. Mary put her best dress on, Jeff looked sideways on in the mirror and patted his tummy, 'not bad.'

They swayed and bumped up the Devil track. The bottom of

the car scraped, the branches scratching on hairpin turns.

The smiling Jackson family were out on the veranda sipping cocktails.

'Come on down,' Steve greeted them. Jeff noticed his white toothed smile, his designer swimwear and Rayban sunglasses, his Blackberry no doubt to keep tabs on his 'Company' he'd been bragging about the night before. Steve poured perfect G&T's, the cubes clinked, 'cheers.' Mary savoured the ice cold bitter sweet; the freezer at dumpsville wasn't cold enough for ice. The kids stripped off and were in the pool, it had room for all of them to dive in and mess around with floats. Jeff tried to ignore Jonny yelling, 'you should see our pool, it's a big puddle.'

Mary couldn't contain herself, 'I'd love a little walk round the garden if that's all right?'

'Course it is, I'll come with you' said Joan.

All Mary wanted was peace and quiet to enjoy the colours and smells, but Joan twittered and squawked, 'of course the children go to private school, I'm terribly involved in the PTA fund raising side of things, cake stalls and what not. Then there's the charity work I do. I hardly have time to catch my breath. I always do home cooking, home grown products, I really haven't a minute. It's wonderful to find this silent paradise to wind down in. What's your villa garden like?'

'Bald and brown.'

'Oh Mary are you a tinsy-winsy bit disappointed in your villa?'

Mary gave Joan a fixed stare before turning away, her face flushed with anger. *What does she know about work, with her charity work.* Mary worked damn hard as a nurse, and the way things were with Jeff's office talking of redundancies, she'd probably be working even harder when she got back.

'Oh dearie me, I think we'd better head back to the boys.' Joan's orange lips puckered.

The "boys" were slugging back beers and slapping huge steaks onto the deluxe barbeque. Mary remembered what fun cooking had been at Marina, and rubbed the various scalds and burns she'd sustained from the primitive stove at Abril.

Steve's voice boomed, 'course I know it was luck, right place, right time, landed on my feet all right with that little lovely.'

Jeff gritted his teeth. Steve had just told him how an inside tip from a friendly banker had quadrupled his income in one fell swoop.

'But isn't that illegal?'

'Oh I don't know about that, you win some you lose some.' Steve winked at Jeff, 'C'mon let's eat.'

Mary had to hand it to Joan, she could cook. She'd done an array of salads, quiches, platters of meat, fish, and the marinades were perfect. There was lots of wine, really good vintage, and the desserts were splendid. The sun set over the veranda, the valley bathed in tassels of pink and orange fringes flickering on the horizon. Mary could have wept.

'Mmmmm this food is lush' said Gina helping herself to thirds.

Steve put his arm round Joan, 'great little cook my Joanie; always puts on a fine spread.'

Mary tried to smile, hating them. Anyone could put on a lavish spread if they had bugger else to do all day.

'Jeff was telling me how precarious his job is, give him another steak there Joanie, might not know where his next meal comes from when he gets back.' Steve laughed, Joan tittered.

Mary made a polite move to leave, she could see Jeff was seething.

'Oh leave the dishes,' Joan waved, 'the maid comes tomorrow.' Another perk of the luxury villa.

Jeff listened to Steve; Steve's success, Steve's golf par, Steve's nudge, nudge, wink wink indiscretions, Steve's bonus; Jeff had a belly full of Steve.

The kids didn't want to leave, 'Oh it's been the best night of the whole holiday.'

'We simply must have another get-together for the children,' Joan gushed.

'Can we come to yours tomorrow ?' Jemima Jackson whined.

Mary blurted 'of course you can'.

'Yeah, you can see how poor people live,' laughed Jonny.

'Don't be so cheeky Jonny, we'll do the best we can.'

'That'd be lovely Mary, thank you.'

Mary forced a smile, as they waved bye.

Jeff drove back very, very slowly. He was getting to know the turns and tricks of the lethal track, he'd worked out how to safely navigate the snaking death trap, but it took some concentration. The kids raved on and on about the Jacksons; it pained Mary and Jeff.

'What will I cook them?' sighed Mary.

'Something poisonous' snarled Jeff.

Mary was glad Jeff felt the same way. 'I feel like the poor relations and they're so damn patronising.'

'Yeah tell me about it.'

Mary did Kebabs and crossed her fingers; the desecrated grill pretending to be a barbeque might or might not work.

'Cooeee' Joan's squeaky voice called out. 'Goodness isn't this a cosy villa?'

Steve shook hands with Jeff, 'Devil of a drive down here, we nearly went over a couple of times, seriously you should complain, it's a death trap, and this place Christ.' Steve laughed.

Joan waltzed round the villa, 'Oh Mary I see what you mean, it's rather primitive isn't it darling?'

Jeff poured drinks for everyone in plastic cups, he ignored the kids scoffing at the pathetic pool. 'No glasses in the cupboard I'm afraid.'

Two rounds of plastic tumblers full of wine later and the meat was barely warmed up. Jeff poured another round and Mary pacified the kids by letting them graze on crisps.

Eventually as the last embers of the barbecue fizzed pfutt, Mary took the kebabs and stuffed them in the oven. She couldn't care less, was pissed and wanted to get bladdered. She wanted this to be over, to be home; to be away from humiliation. She hated Steve and Joan and their indulged brats.

The dodgy thermostat ensured the kebabs were cremated in ten minutes. She apologetically tottered out with the black carcasses. They scavenged what they could swallowing hunks of bread swilled down with more wine.

Everyone woozy, the conversation lurched erratically with no one really following what the other was saying. The kids had eaten all the crisps, there was no dessert; the fridge had stopped working. Another round of drinks sufficed, they let the kids have a lager each. Joan wasn't used to drinking and giggled incessantly, she tried to tell Mary a story but fell off her chair laughing hysterically. Steve was puce, 'Joan's not used to drinking, I think we'd better make a move.' He unsteadily got up, knocking the table, 'come on Joany let's get you home.'

It took both Steve and Jeff to heave her to her feet. When she was upright she flung her arms round Jeff and tried to kiss him. The kids were horrified.

Joan stumbled jammy eyed into Mary slurring schmalz, 'what a loverlee day night.'

They managed to get her into the car singing. Steve stuck his head out of the window and sheepishly thanked them. 'We'll be in touch.' Both knew they wouldn't.

Jeff shook his hand, 'don't forget the track is tricky, you go up about 300 metres then a sharp right, another 300 and a left, another 500 metres and a very sharp left. There's a big tree on the bend so you know exactly where to turn.'

Right oh, let me check that; 300 right, 300 left, 500 sharp left by the big tree.'

'Gotcha.'

Jeff and Mary stood waving until the car was out of sight, the sound of the engine screaming through the air, accelerating. Jeff knew Steve would race; Steve was that kind of guy. Jeff and Mary stood in the dark listening to the revving engine roar. Mary frowned, 'isn't that final bend by the tree right?' She quickly shrugged 'not that it matters.'

The ground shook with a screeching howl of metal ripping

apart. The screams woke the whole valley and the flashing flames of fire were something the locals talked about for years to come.

Footsteps

Beethoven's 5th symphony filled the room, bouncing off glistening walls. The hospital theatre was alive with shadows except for the body spot-lit on the table. A figure in a green surgical gown and mask bent over the patient, eyes fixed on the job in hand. He fit intimately into her, intrigued by the rippling shades; purple, red and pink, a warm wetness, that certain smell. He knew the small tremors and flutters, his fingers licked through the dark. He pulled out, gloves off with a twang. Within ten minutes he was scrubbed up, sliding into latex, ready to cut fresh flesh. Sister Sears unfastened his gown at the end of the list; he gave a brief nod and was gone. She sighed, 'the new doctor seems to be one of those with autistic tendencies, no social graces, just cut and thrust.'

'I think they're taught how to be stuck up twats at medical school,' said staff nurse.

They both laughed.

Doctor Charlotte Burdon banged her fist furiously against the steering wheel. She was stuck as far as she could see in a traffic jam snaking for miles. She drummed her fingers and swept her hair back off her forehead, first day of her new job and she'd be late for her surgical list. This was the job she'd clawed towards for years; poring over text books, dumping boyfriends and a social life. She'd put up with bullying and sexual innuendo from the male dominated world of surgery, and through stubborn determination and driving guts had at last been appointed consultant surgeon. Now on her first day with her own list she was trapped in a seemingly never ending traffic queue. She imagined the raised eyebrows of the staff and smacked the steering wheel again. It was over two hours before the accident was cleared and the traffic could get going. She drove like a bat out of hell, when she eventually arrived at the Infirmary it was late morning.

The Royal Infirmary was an old Victorian building. The austere long corridors stretched round the hospital in long arms, walls painted a greasy yellow as if the building was sick. Charlotte hurried, her footsteps loud on the tiled floor. She briefly stopped at the theatre swing doors, patted her hair and straightened her smart pencil skirt. She held her head high, took a deep breath, and swung the doors open.

The surprised staff were cleaning instruments and smiled a little uncertainly. Sister Sears glanced up from her paperwork 'Hello, can I help you?'

'I'm Doctor Burdon the new surgical consultant, I've got a list this morning.' She slipped her jacket off, business like, ready for action.

'But Doctor Burdon's already done the list.'

'What d'you mean Doctor Burdon's already done the list? I'm Doctor Burdon.'

Sister Sears stared at Charlotte confused, 'the Doctor's already done the operations.'

'Do you mean Doctor Monaghan did my cases because I was delayed?'

'No, no it wasn't Doctor Monaghan, I thought it was…'

The two women faced each other trying to comprehend the situation. After several seconds when neither blinked Charlotte said 'I think we should bleep Doctor Monaghan.'

They waited in the office for Doctor Monaghan who as head of the surgical department had appointed Charlotte. He breezed through the door taking Charlotte's hand. 'Welcome Charlotte, how did the list go?'

Charlotte looked at Nurse Sears and back to Doctor Monaghan 'there seems to have been a mix up this morning.'

Both women relayed their version of events. He listened carefully. Doctor Monaghan had been a surgeon for thirty five years, very little shocked him. 'First of all, who knows about this?'

'Just the three of us' said Sister Sears.

He nodded, 'I suggest we keep it that way. Charlotte you're starting a new job. The last thing you need embarking on your career is the hospital crawling with gutter press. Sister Sears, I'm sure assisting an impostor won't go down well with the nursing management, and I'm due to retire next year and the less fuss about this the better. What was the outcome for the patients by the way?'

Sister Sears shrugged, 'the operations seemed to have been done professionally, I mean no one noticed anything untoward.'

'Could you give a description to the police do you think?'

'I can't honestly say I could, except it was a man's height and build. When I came in he was already gowned and scrubbed up with his mask on. There was no chat or introductions and anyhow he had his classical music on so loud it would've been difficult to have a conversation. The only thing I did notice was he had long thin fingers, even through his surgical gloves I could see that.'

Doctor Monaghan looked from one to the other, 'it could be anyone. An ambitious medical student, a disgruntled doctor, a theatre technician or member of the nursing team.'

Charlotte chipped in, 'someone familiar with theatre life?'

'Exactly. The main thing is no real harm's been done. I realise this isn't the best start to your new job Charlotte, but at the moment I suggest we keep quiet and watch this space.'

Both women agreed with a silent flick of eyes and brief nod.

The next day Sister Sears was polite as was Charlotte, the silent pact sealed.

Charlotte loved working in theatre, under the spotlight, lives held in the balance of her knife. She was in control, it was uncomplicated, you do a good job, the patient gets better. It didn't involve lots of tedious bedside manners, the drudgery of ward work bored her. Charlotte wasn't a team player, she'd be accountable for herself, the others could look after themselves.

She'd worked in umpteen hospitals, from spanking brand new ones with wide foyers and a cold marble nakedness, to crumbly ones like the Infirmary. It yawned and creaked, the lights flickered and dipped, shadows danced, noises echoed.

Charlotte did a lot of on-call. There was a pokey room at the far end of the hospital where she could grab a few hours between cases. Being called out for an emergency used to give her a buzz, it was part of the attraction of surgery, the drama, bursting through the doors to save the day, but since joining the Royal Infirmary instead of excitement she was jumpy. She put it down to anxiety, the long hours and that weird incident on the first day, but she had a constant niggling feeling she was being watched.

The first time she heard the footsteps she'd been walking down the corridor, she turned and it was empty. She started walking again and heard footsteps, she swiveled quickly, no one there. She walked again, only to hear footsteps echoing, she searched the corridor behind her trying a weak 'Hello?' Nothing.

Over the next few weeks it happened so many times she lost count. She began to dread her bleep going off and having to go down the corridors. Charlotte had always been in charge, she dumped boyfriends randomly on a whim, severed contact with friends once they inevitably became boring, and as a kid laughed on the white knuckle rides while all the other kids screamed. This was new territory for her, she was frightened. The footsteps always seemed to get nearer and louder until she could almost feel a cold breath on her neck. When she stopped there was silence. She was aware of her every movement, her breathing. She tried to rationalize the situation; she knew auditory hallucinations were a bad clinical sign, she also knew she wasn't mad.

On-call meant a lot of nights scampering through the corridors, heart pounding. She willed herself not to run, the footsteps only speeded up when she did. One night she also heard a distant rumble. It got louder and louder, Charlotte was rooted to the spot. Round the corner at the end of the corridor the mortuary attendant came into view with his tin can going to pick up the latest fatality. He pushed past her and winked, 'all right pet, you look as if you've seen a ghost.'

Charlotte gave a brittle laugh, 'yes fine, just trying to remember something.'

He rolled on, whistling cheerily.

She called out to him, 'did you pass anyone on this corridor?'

'Only my shadow Doc' he chuckled.

Charlotte's sister Debbie was a practical no nonsense woman. She could tell there was something wrong with Charlotte, who was prickly and short tempered on the phone; usually they could gossip for hours. She pitched up unexpected at Charlotte's flat, a bottle of wine in hand.

Debbie looked round the white clinical space that Charlotte called *home*. 'Oh for God's sake get some nick-nacks, some photos or rugs; anything to make this feel less like a hospital.'

Charlotte sighed, 'I keep meaning to get round to it.'

Debbie popped the cork and handed Charlotte a goldfish bowl glass, 'come on, what's up?'

Charlotte confided in her, furious with herself for letting the situation get to her. 'I can't believe this footsteps business is spooking me, but it's really beginning to bug me.'

Debbie put it into perspective, 'it's some stupid prat playing a sick joke on you. Get a grip girl. You've been head girl, won the prize for surgery, and were top in university surgical exams. You've worked like a Trojan to get to where you are, so don't tell me you're going to let some little underling with a strange idea of practical jokes get to you.'

Charlotte laughed and took a slug of wine, 'I guess you're right.'

'I bet it's some jealous green-eyed creep, or a junior trying to push you off your pedestal. The ridiculous amount of on-call you're doing can't be helping.'

Charlotte smiled, of course Debbie was right.

Debbie topped their glasses up, 'It's bullying in the workplace, ignore it and it'll stop. C'mon cheers, here's to your glittering career.'

The following day Charlotte wore a sharper suit, pointier shoes, redder lipstick. She looked at herself in the mirror. She wouldn't let the bastard get her down.

Her next night on-call she saw the mortuary attendant in the distance, she quickened her steps to keep up with him, the footsteps were loud. Walking with him was better than being alone. It was 3am and the hospital was deserted. He turned to her and grinned, 'on call again Pet?'

'Yes.' She looked at him, 'don't you mind always doing nights?'

'Naw, less hassle, I'm not really a people person.'

'Me neither I suppose, in fact I quite like nights, and the emergency admissions are more interesting than the routine day stuff, it's just the hospital itself…' she bit her lip knowing she sounded pathetic, 'it's a bit spooky down these corridors.'

'Oh Aye, old infirmaries,' he sniffed 'they're always riddled with ghosts.'

Charlotte gave a start, 'you're joking?'

'Well it stands to reason doesn't it? All them folk dying before they're ready.'

Charlotte felt queasy, 'have you ever, y'know, heard anything?'

'Oh Aye' I just get used to them.' He laughed at Charlotte's white face. 'You die if you worry and you die if you don't, so why worry eh?' With that he winked and turned down towards the medical ward to fill his tin can up.

Charlotte watched him push his trolley to the ward wondering how the hell could he enjoy his job so much? She decided he was probably a bit simple. She stepped forward again. There was the faintest echo, then footsteps getting louder. She was going crazy with frustration, there was no answer to this, no control. She'd hardly had any sleep in weeks. She'd already knocked the walls, tapped the floors, craned up at the ceiling and pipes to blame the incessant *tip tap* on some kind of architectural flaw. She knew she was clutching at straws. She went over and over in her head all the people she'd met since starting at the Infirmary, trying to work out who the hell could be doing this. For the hundredth time she couldn't solve it logically.

Charlotte bit her nails, she'd always prided herself on coping, there was no sympathy for namby pamby emotions in her life. She didn't want to ask for help, they'd say she should see a counsellor, she wasn't interested in any touchy-feely *talking* about it. Everyday her nerves were more ragged, and even if she did manage an hour or two of sleep, she woke with footsteps ringing in her ears.

The next night she was called in for a simple appendicectomy. She'd done hundreds before, but was edgy and short-tempered, she'd woken with a start, a cold breath next to her. She got up and dragged herself down the corridors. She passed the mortuary attendant, his eyes were shining 'we're both busy tonight.' He grinned widely.

She hurried on.

Once in the theatre she raggedly bent over the steel sink scrubbing up, her hands shaking. Nurse Sears noticed her trembling and asked gently before the operation, 'are you all right Charlotte? You look a bit pale.'

'Yes yes' she'd snapped.

Minutes later she made the simple sharp slice that severed the artery, within seconds the belly was a gushing sea of blood. There was so much blood pumping it was impossible to see the internal organs. Charlotte's fingers floundered trying to find the artery to clip it and stem the flow. She panicked wading in blindly. 'Get some suction in here now,' she screamed. Her hands uselessly waved up and down as if she was playing the piano, 'I can't locate the source.'

Nurse Sears ran for the suction machine and plunged it into the pooling belly. The tube sucked uselessly against the torrent of red.

The anesthetist yelled, 'he's losing blood pressure, he's going into shock.'

Charlotte jiggled her fingers inside scrabbling for the artery, 'it's impossible, I can't see anything, there's too much blood,' she shook uncontrollably, blood rippled to an ebb and flow while he drowned. He went under and under, and was pronounced dead at 4am.

There was a silence that screamed through the theatre suite. All eyes staring at her; *You killed him.*

She couldn't speak, she turned to stone. There'd be an inquest, she'd be held accountable, she'd be found negligent, she'd be struck off the register. Nurse Sears gently touched her elbow, 'shall I get you a cup of tea?'

Charlotte shook her head and licked her dry lips. Numb and hollow she somehow made her way out of the theatre. She walked down the corridor, the footsteps were quiet and then louder and louder. She turned as she always did to face no one. She waited, very faintly she thought she heard classical music in the distance, she was drawn towards it, nearer and nearer, Beethoven's 5th symphony.

They found her body spread-eagle at the bottom of the stairs. It was whispered she was highly strung, and had reacted badly to the terrible tragedy of losing one of her patients.

The whole episode was hushed up, and within weeks was sewn into the tapestry of hospital folklore and gossip. The wheels of hospital life turned as usual, the doctors and nurses and porters went about their business, while the grinning mortuary attendant efficiently collected his bounty in his long thin fingers.

THE FAR ROOM

MUM TAKES US THROUGH A BUSHY GARDEN. THERE ARE dandelions with puffs of fluff, and green weeds tangle round my knees. I hold Mum's hand a bit tighter. 'This used to be such a neat garden, I remember visiting it as a little girl about your age Maeve. Great Grandma's house is going to be our new home, isn't that exciting?'

The porch is covered in cobwebs. Andy pulls them apart with a stick he found in the garden. I pull his sleeve, 'Andy don't, spiders might come after us at night crawling over our beds for revenge...'

'Don't be silly Maeve.' Mum gives me one of her cross looks. She unlocks the peeling red front door, it creaks open with a push.

Mum takes us round big empty rooms, tall ceilings, thick doors. It has a creaky staircase that goes up and up. We follow her. In the bathroom there's a bell on the wall. 'That was for when you needed to call the maid to help you out of the bath,' says Mum pressing it. We hear it ring downstairs.

'Where's the shower?'

'It doesn't have one, but it will.'

The rooms have long tall windows. At our old house they were wide and square and I could reach them. I have a fluttery feeling in my tummy, I swallow down. I'm sad I won't be able to look out those windows anymore.

Mum leads us across the landing to the bedrooms. She pushes a door open, 'this is going to be the girls' room.' She means my big sisters.

I walk into a big bright room, it has two windows and the sun pours in. Me and Andy stamp loud on the bare floorboards. Mum laughs and dances us out into a green room, 'and this room's going to be yours Andy.'

It's a cosy room snuggled between the girls' and Mum and Dad's room. It feels warm and safe, he likes it. Mum leads us on, 'and this is mine and Dad's room.' This is a big room, it feels like a grown ups room.

'So where will I sleep Mum?'

'Ah well that's a surprise, follow me.' She takes us back onto the landing where there's a corridor with a dark wiggly staircase going up. At the top of the stairs it has a room, one room only. We peek into an oblong box of a room. I shiver; a cold room.

'This room will be lovely once it's decorated don't you think Maeve?'

'I don't know.'

'Well you can have this lovely little room all to yourself, lucky you.'

'It's a long way from all of you… I'm not sure I like it.'

'Well I'm sorry young lady. Really, you don't know how lucky you are.'

She acts like I've pushed a present she's given me back in her face. She turns and goes down, her feet sound loud on the stairs. Andy pokes me.

My sisters spend loads of time in their room. I tip toe round them, trying to be liked. Sometimes they let me in their lovely room, most of the time they don't. They paint it pink and white, all strawberries and cream. One afternoon they let me watch them practice with make-up and even ask me a few times which looks nicest. At last and I'm brave enough to ask, 'would either of you like to swap rooms?'

'You're joking? It's not a proper room, it doesn't even have a proper wardrobe.'

'It has Grandpa's trunk, Mum says she's going to clean it out and I can keep my clothes in there.'

'It's spooky that trunk, I wouldn't have it in the same room as me.'

I get that fluttery feeling, and leave their pink room. I don't even try with Andy. I know he won't give up his room next to Mum and Dad, he has all his posters and model planes up.

I wander into the garden because it's difficult to know where to go when nowhere feels like home. I hate my room. It's cold, even though they give me a heater to plug in. The far room, that's what we call it.

My room is the only room that you can hear the sea in. Mum says I'm lucky. I like the sea a lot, but it sounds very loud in my room. The sound makes me tired, the waves going back and forth. I feel heavy, I sink under the waves and every day drift further and further away.

At night I can't sleep in my room, I lie awake hearing the sea. When I do fall asleep it's a foggy sleep like a sea mist, and I wake early every morning still tired.

In the mornings Dad gets up before everyone else, but I'm so worried I'll drown in my sleep I've been getting up earlier and earlier. One morning I'm up before him and I think I give him a bit of a fright sitting at the table watching the sunshine wake up.

'What's wrong with you Maeve?' He sits next to me, and puts his arm round my shoulder. I don't mean for it to happen but big heavy drops roll down my cheeks. 'I don't like my room.'

He doesn't give me "a look" but is nice. 'Why darling?'

I can't say *the sea is going to wash me away* or *it feels like you want to get rid of me* or *it makes me feel lonely*. I'm trying to be grown up. So I say, 'it's very cold and dark.'

Dad pulls me on his knee and brushes my hair back. 'C'mon darling, it's not that bad. How about if we decorate it? Whatever colours you want eh? And you could have a sleepover.'

'Yes I'd like that.' I know I'm kidding myself. It'll be like putting a plaster on a wasp sting, it'll still hurt underneath, but I don't want to upset Dad, and I hardly ever get to sit on his knee nowadays.

My sisters do most of the painting. We do it white, so I can put posters and pictures up. They give me a brush, but say I can only do the skirting board; the bits that don't really matter. When it's painted it feels like a white coffin instead of a dark one. The sea's still very loud. My bed's a ship sailing further and further away.

In the morning I sit playing with my cornflakes because I don't feel hungry nowadays.

'Maeve for goodness sake look at you. You should be ready for school, I don't believe you've brushed your hair in days, and your uniform's dirty. Go upstairs and put a fresh one on. I don't know what's the matter with you.'

I drag myself upstairs but my legs are heavy, filled with sand. It seems hard work doing the buttons again, trying to fasten my skirt. I look at myself in the mirror to do my hair. I don't look like me. I don't smile.

'C'mon Maeve we're going to be late, have you brushed your teeth?'

'Yes.' We both know I'm lying. I get *a look*.

On Friday Mrs Sproggart gives me a letter. 'Give it to your Mother Dear.'

'Did no one else get one, what's it about?'

'I dunno, she sealed it.'

I watch Mum's eyes follow the words. She gives a big sigh and says, 'Andy can you go out and play please.'

'Has Maeve been naughty?'

'Mind your own business, go on hoppit.'

Mum asks me to sit down opposite her at the kitchen table. 'Maeve, Mrs Sproggart thinks you aren't very happy, you're not joining in at class. What's the matter, have you fallen out with Julie?'

'No.' I wish I was sitting next to her and that she'd put her arm round me.

'Is someone bullying you?'

'No'

'Well what is it darling?'

I feel bad for making her worried. She's been so busy, she has a flick of paint in her hair from decorating and putting furniture in the house and straightening it up. I take a big breath and decide to tell her about the room swallowing me up, taking me out to sea, but then she says, 'this all seems to have happened since we moved house, it's so silly Maeve we have a lovely house, and everyone else is so happy. Why aren't you?'

I can't tell her, it'd be spoiling everyone else's happiness, and I know I'd get *a look*. So instead I say, 'I think I'm tired Mum, the sea's so loud in my room it keeps me awake…'

'Oh Maeve, not that ridiculous business again.' She throws her tea-towel on the table and stands up to stir something on the cooker with her back to me. 'I just don't know what to do with you.'

My eyes are watery. I'm glad she can't see; it'd make her more annoyed.

That night the dark swirls over me. Waves and whirls, a scarf wrapping round, I can't breathe. I get out of bed and lie outside my quilt. It's cold but I don't get inside because I might fall asleep, and if I fall asleep I'll be washed out to sea. I know the sea will swallow me if I don't do something soon.

The next morning I fall asleep at the kitchen table. Andy laughs because my hair falls in the cornflakes. Mum helps me to stand up, 'come on Maeve, back to bed, I think you should miss school today.'

'Please can I get in your bed?'

'Oh okay, just this once.'

I snuggle in. It smells of Mum and Dad, it's safe. I can hear the house living; the heating, Mum clattering dishes, the radio on. Mum comes up about an hour later. She picks up clothes and moves the perfumes and smelly stuff around on her dressing table. I feel sleepy but want to make the most of having her to myself. 'Mum isn't it weird that this is the house your Great Grandparents lived in, tell me about them.'

She sits on the edge of the bed, and it's lovely because it seem ages since Mum has had time to talk to me, not since we've been in this house, and had all the *straightening* to do.

'Great Grand Dad I hardly knew. All I remember he was a big man who sat by the fire staring into the flames. He never said much. He was a seafarer, that's why he had the big trunk. He died at sea, in a storm.'

My heart jumps, 'I didn't know that.'

'Well that kind of thing happened a lot then. Great Grandma was shattered and died of a broken heart soon after.'

Then Mum describes the house when she'd visited it as a little girl. 'It was beautiful Maeve, and when we're finished here, it'll be even more beautiful. You'll love it then, especially your room.'

I'm glad my eyes are heavy, that I'm falling to sleep, her voice drifting over me instead of the sea. I don't want Mum's eyes not to sparkle with imagining the house. I'm glad to fall asleep so I don't spoil it all by hating that room.

She must've left, and the day is gone. It's a good heavy sleep, the sort I used to have at our old house. I liked our old house that was modern and small. It didn't creak and yawn, was bright pastels instead of dark wood, and I never felt alone in that house. Here I'm a speck of sand that'll be blown away.

I'm very frightened that night so in the very darkest bit of night, when the blackness is trying to sniff me out, I get my sleeping bag and creep down my creaky stairs to the bathroom. I put the sleeping bag in the bottom of the bath, with my quilt on top. It's not very comfy but I can see the light from the landing and feel safer. The lapping sea can't reach me here, the trunk can't open up; I sleep. The next morning I hear Dad get up for a wee. I hurry back up to the room before he comes into the bathroom. I decide to do this every night. I'll be safer.

Grandma's there when I get in from school. I throw myself into her, smelling her perfume and hearing beads jangle as she hugs me. I love Grandma and her softness, I love her more than anything because she loves me, even if I'm silly. Mum says 'would you like to show Grandma round the house Maeve?'

I do it like a tour guide… 'And this is the where the family relax in the lounge…and this is where they take their meals…' I leave *that* room until the end which is easy as it's so far away. Finally, I pull her by the hand round and up the stairs. I look at Grandma, 'and this is nobody's room.'

Grandma looks at me, her eyes have flecks of yellow in the brown. 'And who's room is it?'

'It's meant to be mine, but it shouldn't be. I'm drowning in it.' I kick the wall hard.

She puts her arm round me. 'Maeve what do you mean darling?'

'In my head Grandma, the sea in my head is pulling me under, every night I go deeper. It's a different sea….' I whisper, 'I'm drowning.'

'Oh Maeve' she laughs, 'you are a drama Queen, we'll have to get you on the stage.' She pulls me close, 'I'll perhaps have a word with your Mum. Things can seem very strange when you move house.'

I listen through the banister, 'Oh Mum if it wasn't her room it'd be something else. I really don't think we should pander to her, you know what an imagination she has, she'll settle, it's early days yet.'

When Grandma's getting ready to go back to London she says, 'next time I come to visit I'm going to sleep, and I'm going to stay in your room with you.'

'Oh please do that Grandma soon.' But I know Grandma lives a long way away and she's old. It might be ages before she comes again. I might be dead by then.

For two nights I creep to the bathroom and make my little bed in the bath. I hear Dad get up for his morning wee, and hurry back before he comes in the bathroom, but on the third night I sleep through the toilet flush, and he finds me.

'Maeve this is ridiculous, this cannot go on.'

At breakfast Mum bangs cupboards and pans, I know she's very angry. 'Maeve no more pocket money until you stop being so silly.'

Andy kicks me under the table and pretends it's an accident.

No one talks on the drive to school, Mum doesn't even say 'Bye'. At the school gates I bend down pretending to tie my shoelaces, until I see Mum turn the corner to go back home. Andy races into the playground and when I get up, I turn away from the school gates, and just keep on walking. I walk and walk, and turn the corner, and then another corner. I walk and walk, it sounds as if the sea's calling me, and I follow. When I get there I walk along the shore. I don't feel alone for the first time in ages, I listen to the whispers. I pass an old man with a beard, he's wrinkled like a peach stone, I wonder if he's Great Grand dad. I walk all day, and never stop walking, looking out at the sky.

They find me later that evening, just as the sea and the sky become one big, dark blue. I don't want to talk, so I don't.

They talk of trauma, and shock, and possibly epilepsy. Then after seeing lots of doctors after lots of weeks they decide it's a virus. Mum moves me onto a little bed in their room, they don't know when I'll be better. I'm weak as a kitten, and can't eat much, or do very much. They say it can take a long time, nobody knows why or how it happens. There is no treatment.

I think I'll have it until I'm a grown up, then they can't make me sleep in the far room.

Cuckold

Karen snivelled into the hankie the policeman gave her. 'He was about five foot ten, stocky, tanned, smart looking and well spoken, that's what surprised me most, not like you'd imagine a… '

'You're doing really well Karen, I know this has all been a terrible shock.' The policewoman patted her hand reassuringly, 'try to keep focused on his description while it's fresh in your mind.'

'Sorry' she snivelled again, 'not every day you get a gun pointed in your face.'

'Don't worry we'll catch him, that's for certain. Carry on,' she urged.

'He had very blue eyes, and a nice smile. I can't remember anything else.'

Karen cried loudly, it had shaken her up. It wasn't what you expected when you went to work on a Monday morning. The police were nice to her but she was befuddled with all their questions, she tried to remember how was his hair parted? Left or right? Was it brown or perhaps grey? Maybe he'd been taller, you don't take much notice dealing with people all day as a bank clerk. She hoped she'd look good in the Evening papers and wished she'd washed her hair that morning.

He'd walked in cocksure, right up to her counter, smiling with his cheque book ready. She'd glanced up, a Mister nobody. He could wait until she'd finished counting '*Just a moment please*' she'd said keeping her head down. When she did look he was grinning with a gun pointing straight at her, less than one meter away. He was done and dusted in seconds, there was no time to think except to do exactly as he asked, hand all the money over. Thick wads efficiently packed away in his briefcase. He clicked it shut, eyes teasing, 'have a nice day.' He'd shoot from outside the building if she moved. He watched her through the glass like he said he would. She'd smiled back; he'd told her to. She grinned inanely, rigid with fear blinking back tears until he was out of sight.

Eddie was a tidy guy. He took care of his personal grooming, took care of himself. He wore good after-shave and co-ordinated his clothes, he liked what he saw in the mirror. He had a couple of friends but wasn't one for the pub, hating hangovers, hating not being in control. He went to the fitness club three times a week finishing up on the sun-bed to top up his golden brown. He liked fast cars, designer sunglasses, sushi and shopping. He didn't like reading, theatre, or people who wanted to save the planet. He was non-smoking, healthy eating and slept well. He opened doors with a smile, and would chat about the weather. He believed image was everything, any fool could see that, you only had to look at Posh and Becks. Andrea his wife kept him on his toes, whether to tuck his shirt in or to leave it out of his designer trousers. She insisted they were seen in the right restaurants, and hobnobbed with the golf club crowd, her ambition in life to be admitted to the inner sanctum of the ladies team.

Eddie worked in production for a perfume company. He'd been there ten years, it was routine and boring but secure. Before he met Andrea he'd had a few girl friends, but never felt committed, he wasn't one for one-night stands; he had an excessive fear of sexually transmitted diseases. When Andrea, the new sales representative walked through the door she was the dream he'd been waiting for strutting past his desk, in one glance she swallowed him up without chewing.

A bully by nature, Andrea revelled in his exaltation. She crossed her legs on the pedestal he lifted her up to and felt good. She demanded expensive meals and clothes, he showered her with gifts, she wore sharp chic suits, black and white with a slash of colour, it made co-ordinating simple. She measured her calorie intake, kept her figure trim, a cream cake with lunch and she'd forfeit tea. Her life was balanced and measured. Days at the hair salon, days for her body wax, days for her facial mud pack. Eddie was perfect, he'd been promoted recently and could give her the suburbia lifestyle she craved as an addict to Hello magazine. She was young, a lot younger than Eddie and with time on her side, she gave their marriage a seven year prognosis, then divorce with a nice settlement, she didn't believe in love and a whole life with steady Eddie was even less believable. She had higher aspirations, and marriage was easier than getting on *The Apprentice*. This was a stop-gap, they'd rub along nicely, a waiting room relationship.

Eddie sometimes wondered if he should want more from life, neither wanting children, nor having a driving passion for anything; a hankering to own a Porche he guessed didn't count. Duncan from marketing gave up half his life savings to charity after watching 'Comic Relief.' Eddie noticed Duncan seemed lighter and happier after, as if money had been weighing him down. Duncan handed his notice in a few months later and left to do VSO in Africa. He said that night in alone watching snatches of dying Africans between Dawn French and Chris Moyles belly bouncing jokes was his epiphany. Eddie sniffed and didn't think too deep about it, it wasn't worth the heartache, and anyhow, Andrea hated Comic Relief, she found poverty distasteful.

Their years of suburbia ran into each other with little rippling, Andrea kept busy decorating their mock Tudor house, it was co-ordinated and clean, everything had its place, Eddie tried not to look untidy. He'd do what she told him to do, clean the car, mow the lawn, paint the fence, anything for an easy life.

When the merger took place that had been gossiped about for

months as the recession bit deeper, he took no notice. It was whispered down the corridors, rumours rattled on the tea trolley and futures flirted with at the Christmas office parties. Eddie had got past the sweaty insecure stage where juniors found their futures freed up on a Monday morning.

Maybe it was because it was so unexpected, or maybe he was in shock, but when Eddie lost his job he pretended he hadn't. The company were down-sizing, something to do with new technology, he was dispensable and had be dispensed with. He walked out of the company, no handshake but a pat on the back and good luck. He was unemployed, without an income, in his shirt and tie up shit creek without a paddle. He went home at the normal time, cooked their tea, chatted to Andrea about where to put the new patio heater and didn't tell a soul.

For the next three months he kissed her turned back and went to the cafe in town. He'd sit scouring the jobs pages over a cup of coffee he could make last an hour. Then he'd move onto the library. It was quiet and warm, he'd stay all day. He gave up his membership of the leisure club, he couldn't afford any luxuries. After doing his sums he reckoned he had six months of survival money before the bailiffs came knocking or kicking the door down. He knew he'd get sorted before then, something would come along, there was no need to bother Andrea with it all. He pretended to go to the fitness club as usual, he'd run out to the car in his gym gear, drive round the corner and park on the next street; not wanting to use much petrol. He'd run for the hour he should've been at the gym and then go home to tell her who he'd seen at the club, she barely listened to him anyhow.

He felt he was still in control if no-one knew, he'd get back on his feet before anyone knew, Andrea especially, must never know.

While he pounded the streets in his work outs, he'd go over and over interviews in his head, where they'd gone wrong. He'd had hundreds, and as many disappointments. His CV lacked IT skills, lacked experience, lacked qualifications. The fact that there was a recession and others out there in the same boat, didn't soften the blow. His hair was thinning, worry left fuzzy patches of anxious pink scalp. Andrea didn't like it, 'Oh go and get a hair transplant or some drug off the internet, you look a mess, you haven't the cheekbones to carry off baldness.'

Eddie didn't expect kindness or understanding from Andrea, they weren't like that. They'd be fine as long as he got another job, he'd get back on his feet. She wouldn't understand if he told her, she wanted a Gazebo, something would turn up, he'd get it sorted, soon he'd be back on track.

He'd started waking up weeks ago. Cold sweat ran in rivers down his fast fading tan. He'd get up, careful not to wake her and have a shower. Sometimes he slumped against the shower wall, sliding down and stayed in the cubicle, feeling safe under the hot pouring water. Then he'd sit in the kitchen and watch the sun rise, to carve up another day for him. Oh Jesus another day. He'd pace the floor, it was twenty two steps across, fourteen steps wide, he knew his world was shrinking, options were closing down.

Another day for another set of bills to drop on the front door mat, for him to sweep them up, unopened, to hide them before Andrea swam down in her fluffy negligee. Another day he'd peck her goodbye, and set off in his grey suit and tie to trudge to his cafe and sit. They let him stay all morning now, as long as it was in the front window so he made the place look busy. He turned the spoon over in his empty cup, counted grains of sugar; sand through a timer and his time had run out. There were no more options, his world imprisoned him. He thought about Duncan, the concept of free will and hope hovered in his conscience. Maybe he could start again, come clean, do something meaningful, but Eddie couldn't think of anything he fancied with *meaning* and Andrea's disgust of "do gooders" made Duncan evaporate from his mind. Eddie gripped the formica table, he'd get some control over this situation yet.

There was no money left, no shares to cash in, no more jewellery to pawn, no hidden pots of gold to dip into. He put his head on the table crushed under an avalanche of anxiety.

It was a plan driven by desperation. His plan, no one else involved to screw it up.

He got the gun from Fenwick's toy department for 2.99p. It fooled her. She did as she was told, no messing. She boosted his confidence, she'd do anything he wanted. It was easy, he didn't mind scaring her, she thought he was dangerous; he was back in control and that's all that mattered. Within ten minutes he was rich, the fat wads ran into thousands. Maybe now he could even sleep again.

He bought a bottle of champagne on the way home. Andrea sniffed and said 'Yeah all right I'll have glass, what are we celebrating?'

The doorbell went as the champagne cork popped, he put the bottle down, 'won't be a tick.'

Two policemen faced him, 'we'd like you to accompany us to the station to help with our enquiries.'

Andrea was standing behind him, she fluttered her eyelids at the taller officer, Eddie noticed she'd put fresh lipstick on.

Eddie went willingly with the police officer, still unable to tell the truth.

The tall police officer came back later and explained everything. When she heard what had happened, how Eddie lost his job, Andrea laughed out loud. When she heard of his pretending to go to work every day, she rolled chortling, when she heard how he robbed a bank, her sides ached in hysterical shrieks. She listened amazed to how he almost got away with it, scot free, the lone Ranger, but guffawed uncontrollably into her handkerchief when she heard that a customer noticed his cheque book left on the counter and kindly handed it in, the tears rolled in glee, she giggled and wiped her eyes. 'How on earth did a smart girl like me marry such a loser?' She asked the tall policeman, her eyes widening while she stroked his arm with her beautifully manicured hands.

They understood one another, immediate gratification wasn't to be sniffed at, soon he was unzipping as she was slipping out of her silk blouse, they were careful not to smudge her new settee that matched the curtains.

Andrea and Eddie had been married almost seven years.

Festive Greetings

Adrionis was full of Christmas parties. To their left was a gaggle of hairdressers shooting party poppers, to their right a table of nurses swapping ward stories, cackling and hooting.

'So much for a quiet romantic meal,' sighed Joanne.

Jeff reached across and squeezed her hand, 'Sweetheart, you know there's nothing I want more than for us to be together at Christmas, but I can't. Susie's not very robust, I think she'd have a complete break-down if I left her now, and there's the kid's to think of.'

'You've been leaving her since I met you.'

'You've been wonderfully patient Jo, it won't be long, I promise you, but now's not the right time, I think she'd do something silly.' He squeezed her hand, 'you're so understanding, it's one of the reason's I love you.'

Joanne nodded, of course he had to spend Christmas with *her* and the two kids, it wouldn't be right to do otherwise.

Joanne would go home for Christmas and listen to her Mum fret and sigh, 'will you ever settle down and give me a grandchild?'

Dad would offer hourly Emva cream sherries, 'after all, it is

Christmas' he'd chortle.

They'd have a rolled turkey breast from M&S; a full turkey was too much. The last time they'd had one it sat plumply lasting days. It was a relief not to have the marathon of turkey leftovers disguised in various gooey sauces.

Joanne was a good daughter and would titter at her cracker jokes. She'd put on her silly paper hat and grin, while Dad worked out puzzles for ten year olds. The three of them would whoop and create a hullabaloo while Dad poured brandy over the Christmas pudding and set it alight. They'd ignore the strange paraffin taste clinging, and pluckily munch through. They'd have a liquor while listening to the Queen. Mum liked Baileys and Dad'd have a whiskey. Normally Joanne would have both to help get through the day. Dad's head would be a shiny bauble, he liked Christmas; easily pleased. When Joanne was a teenager she worked out she'd been conceived at Christmas. The thought horrified her and she'd looked at her parents in disbelief; every year her conception hovered amidst the holly and mince pies.

She could usually escape on Boxing Day as John Lewis started their sale then, and she'd be due back at work. She was second in command in the Accessories Department. Her Mum seemed to imagine she was a Company Director, and would tut 'oh don't be so modest,' bragging about her *career daughter* and 'what our Joanne doesn't know about belts and scarves isn't worth knowing.'

Every year her Mum would take her aside with motherly advice. 'Now don't forget, all work and no play makes Jill a dull girl.' And 'how are you going to meet a nice young man if you're always working?'

Dad would put his hands in his pocket and rock back and forth on his heels, 'Auntie Jean'll be disappointed you can't make it to her Boxing Day 'do'.

'Me too' Joanne would mutter, 'give them all my love.' Relieved she'd have none of the *On your own still Joanne*? and *Met anyone nice yet*? or *When are you going to settle down?*

Every year her Mum and Dad would cuddle her on the doorstep, clinging to her arms, she'd have to peel herself away to escape. They'd blow kisses until she drove out of sight, away from their matchstick figures waving disappointment.

Tina from Lingerie in the adjacent aisle to Accessories loved Christmas. She'd begin countdown in September drumming her long fingernails on the counter, 'Oh God Joanne, I've so many people to buy for I don't know where to start.' Then she'd begin writing out lists, which stretched on for days. 'So many cards to send, too many people to buy for; still that's what Christmas is about eh?' Her busy fingers would dance up and down her computer keyboard, manic cockroaches click-it y clack, searching for the *perfect* presents.

Tina looked like a Christmas cracker all year round. She wore bright glittery clothes with tight waisted belts; she ballooned out from either side. With her blonde fuzzy hair she was a popped champagne bottle. She was great in Sales, buttering customers up, especially the perplexed men buying a little festive something for their partners. They'd be tentatively fingering the itsy bitsy black and red impractical pieces of string until Tina would gently steer them away from the boned basques towards softer silk and satins. 'Comfort matters too' she'd smile with the confidence of a whorish big sister who'd been around a while. She'd get them to describe their wives to her so she could help choose what might be the most flattering style for them. It never ceased to amaze Tina how many blokes imagined their wives would fit into tiny weany size 8 thongs. She always felt a twinge of failure after Christmas as a long line of plump women queued up to exchange their ridiculous micro knickers for something that went further up than their big toe.

In-between successful sales Tina would be dashing hither and thither buying pressies. She was often popping into Accessories, once every day at least with 'do you think pink is too young for a middle aged Aunt? I've got Steve's mother to buy for too, I really don't know what to get her, she has everything.'

Steve was Tina's partner, he was a lawyer. Tina always came to Joanne to buy a dickie bow alongside a million other little goodies for him. 'He's such a poser' she'd smile fondly choosing the most *please notice me* dickie bow in the shop. Tina made it be known she didn't need to work but got bored. 'And anyhow I get under the cleaner's feet when I'm at home.' She'd twiddle a pen, adding to her list as she was talking.

Accessories was manic at Christmas, lots of ladies shopped for scarves that would almost certainly be relegated to the back of drawers by Boxing Day. Like Tina, so many of them seemed to be frantic '*doing*'. They'd mix and match, co-ordinate and contrast. Their eyes darted, hands stretching and touching, feeling and grasping. Joanne sighed, she always felt as if she stood outside Christmas; watching it rah-rah by.

Around November Tina would start fretting about her dress for the Christmas party. 'Have you got your dress yet Joanne?'

'Not yet.'

'Well purple is this year's black and Karen Millen have this lush dress to die for.'

'Why don't you buy it then?'

'Steve's already bought me a French Salon outfit. It cost hundreds, I have to wear it, it'd be rude not to, but I'll take you at lunch to try the purple dress on.'

'But....'

'No buts, it'll take us twenty minutes, it's only on the next floor. C'mon Jo let your hair down, it'll be fun.'

Joanne squeezed into the maroon boob tube. She turned sideways. 'I look five months pregnant.'

'Nothing a pair of magic knickers can't sort out.' A torture device, Joanne bought the lot to keep Tina quiet, she'd sneak them back the next day.

Joanne hated the work Christmas party. They stood around with glasses of cava, giggling shop mannequins come to life for one night only. It was like a school end of term party, all dressed up and nowhere else to go. Joanne watched normal functioning human beings become predators after a couple of drinks, stalking and eventually going for the kill with tongues down each other's throats. She glanced over at Tina laughing with Mike from Accounts, how did she enjoy everything in life so much? Mike was as much fun as watching paint dry. Joanne studied Tina for a minute or two. She wasn't particularly pretty, and certainly didn't have the best of figures, but she was so lively, so full of fun. Joanne wondered how she always managed to look on the bright side of life. Joanne nodded to whatever dreary Margery from Haberdashery was whining on about and soon slipped her cava into a discrete corner and left early as usual. She'd be on hand in the morning for the post-party counselling sessions in the coffee room. Poor spotty Kevin the young temporary lad from Linens was the worst casualty. He came in the next morning after brushing his teeth so hard his gums were bleeding. 'I can't believe what happened' he said dazed.

Joanne gave him a strong sugary coffee. Shakily he'd sipped it from chapped lips, 'her feather boa was like a snake round me.'

Joanne nodded understanding. She'd seen Gloria from Confectionaries stick her toffee arms round him and knew he'd never escape. Kevin swallowed a fistful of vitamins to get through the day. The shame of snogging fifty year old fat Gloria pained him, not helped by Julie, Gloria's side-kick passing round photos of them caught in action.

'Think of it as character building.' Joanne patted Kevin's hand and moved onto sobbing Trudi who'd woken up next to her boss; big mistake.

Joanne's Christmas shopping was predictable. Tie and socks for Dad, scarf for Auntie Jean, smellies for Mum. She usually bought something for the girls working on her counter too, something like Body lotion; a gesture really. The present she liked doing the most was a shoe box for an orphan somewhere in the world. You could choose girl or boy; she chose girl. She spent hours prettying it with ribbons and girlie bows. She imagined her orphan opening it up, eyes widening, her face lighting up, smiling ear to ear with excitement. Joanne went to a lot of trouble filling her shoebox. Alongside luxury sweeties would be glittery jewellery, bangles and beads, bubble bath, a hair band, some lacy topped socks, a pen and pencil set and a little diary with pictures of kittens in it. She'd wrap it up carefully in pink rustling paper and matching bows. She'd keep it on the coffee table after she'd got it ready, leaving it there for at least a week. She liked it being there when she got in from work, reminding her of the delight it would give the little girl. Even on Christmas Day she'd think of the child opening the box and lifting the presents out one by one, hugging them. It made Joanne's day a bit brighter.

Joanne met Tina in the jewellery section while buying the bangles.

'Oh Joanne, thank goodness a sensible person to help me choose, otherwise I might buy up the whole shop, I love them all. What do you think of these for my thirteen year old niece?' She held up some multicoloured six inch long dangly earrings.

'She'd need to be quite a confident teenager to wear them.'

Tina held them against Joanne, 'Hmmm I think they might be a bit much for Katy's Mum. Families eh?'

Joanne wished she was from a big family; a big gregarious loving family with brothers and sisters and lots of cousins and aunties and uncles and laughter. The rest of the year Joanne felt okay, normal even, but Christmas she was deficient somehow; inadequate. She thought of helping out at a soup kitchen, she'd like the camaraderie and the feeling of belonging but it'd break Mum and Dad's heart, so she never did it.

Jeff had less time to see her over Christmas what with Christmas plays and kids parties. They argued a lot, she didn't know where their relationship was going, he bleated platitudes and she told him to piss off.

That was the pattern since they'd met. He'd skulk round sheepishly after the festivities were over. He'd bring some big *sorry* present, an expensive necklace or bracelet, never a ring. He'd kiss her passionately saying he couldn't live without her. Then they'd have hot sex and stare into each other's eyes agreeing somehow they'd work it out. He'd kiss her face again and again, 'Darling let's never argue again.'

Joanne knew she should ditch him, but didn't have the strength to face the loneliness. She had some good friends, enjoyed their company, but their lives were on the move; getting married, having kids, changing jobs, travelling the world, while she was going nowhere.

Tina's life whizzed the fastest; eating out, Christmas parties and decorating every inch of the department with tinsel and sparkles. 'Don't you just love Christmas decorations?' and with that she broke into song, singing alongside the festive medley that played again and again in the store, '*Oh I wish it could be Christmas everyday….*'

'What you doing for Christmas Joanne?'

'Going home.' She hoped the conversation would stop there.

'How many will be there?' asked Tina while tying an extravagant bow on a box, her tongue slightly protruding in concentration.

'Just the three of us, I'm from a small family.'

Tina frowned, 'well thank your lucky stars, I'll be exhausted by the time it's all over. There's fifteen of us this year, Steve and my family together, you can barely hear yourself speak, good job I'm a natural fog horn eh?' She smacked her lips and started on another parcel.

On Christmas Eve Joanne hugged and wished *Happy Christmas* to all her colleagues. It would only be two days and she'd be seeing them again, but it was a before and after life. She walked past the lingerie department, and noticed a bag bulging with sparkly wrapped presents. She knew they were Tina's, she must've forgotten them. She picked the bag up; it was a time of goodwill; she looked up her address, it wasn't that far out of her way, she'd drop them off on the way home. She left the store waving bye and stepped into the city streets. The shops were closed, the streets quiet, everyone had hurried home to their loved ones. Joanne liked this time, the misty chill, the streets glistening with glimmering frosty festive lights, the peace of a city at rest. She walked to her car slowly, Mum would have ham and mash ready, it was their traditional Christmas Eve meal. Dad would be fumbling the sherry stopper. She looked up at the stars and sighed; she had good health, enough money, a secure job; she was better off than many. She walked slowly, trying to analyse why she always felt miserable at Christmas. Next year she would do the soup kitchen, and next week she was going to dump Jeff, she was sick of watching the world go by. If she was Tina she'd be laughing and chatting, maybe setting an extravagantly laid table, or circulating at a fancy cocktail party. She hoped Tina would be in when she dropped the presents off, maybe she'd invite her in and introduce her to her exciting friends.

A beggar huddled in a doorway as Joanne got to her car. She rummaged in her bag and handed him a fiver, 'Happy Christmas.'

She could still hear him shouting, 'Merry Christmas, God bless you' as she drove away.

Tina had left the department store, cheerily waving festive wishes. She got a taxi home and climbed the stairs up to her third floor bedsit. She unlocked the door and stepped into silence. She lay her bags down on the bed alongside the other huge pile of gifts. She'd take them to a charity shop in January, that's what she always did. She kicked off her shoes, undid her tight belt and slumped on the sofa in a fugue, the tears flowing freely, her fixed smile washed away.

After a while she slowly opened the gift the department store gave to all its workers as a small thank you. It was a jar of brandy butter; she stuck her finger in and licked it. As a kid it'd been a jar of sweeties. She used to tell everyone they were from her Mum and Dad, that they'd be coming to collect her soon. After a while she believed it herself; she was good at pretending.

Tina got up to answer the door wearily; probably the kid's downstairs again messing around.

Joanne waited listening to the door chain being unhooked. Tina didn't live in the sort of flat she'd imagined she would.

The two women faced each other; Tina red-eyed and blotchy, Joanne's smile fading as she held the forgotten bag of presents out to her, 'Happy Christmas.'

Bird Flu

Hawk sat head of the board room table. He stroked a whorl while waiting for the twittering cawing to calm, for their rustling papers to settle. He liked to feel the wood under his long fingers. His face twitched, he scratched his nose watching them, beady eyes flicking, he didn't miss a trick. Eventually they stilled and looked up at him anxiously. He reached for his paper with a tanned sinewy arm, 'shall we begin?'

The world powers were meeting to discuss the bird flu crisis. Hawk presented the problems to them which were escalating. Up until now the United States of America had ignored bird flu; after all it wasn't in their back yard. They adopted the Ostrich position, heads deep in the sand. In the past Hawk had little time for bird flu, as far as he could see it was a Chinkie slitty-eyed problem. Folk who were base enough to sleep with their birds were asking for trouble. Even when it spread to Europe he wondered could this be evolutionary selection; nature weeding out the weaklings. Hawk believed that AIDS was put on this earth by the good Lord to rid the world of all the Queers and too highly sexed Africans who'd get their end away with the mere sight of a skirt blowing in the breeze. All those hippy junkies too, spreading their legs in the name of *free* love. Christ did we really want that sort on the planet? No sirree, Mother Nature was a cunning Dude. Of course Hawk had learnt to keep his opinions to himself, political correctness had gone crazy. He sighed knowing it wouldn't be long before some animal rights activists would be waving their scrawny vegan arms round, throwing nut cutlets in defiance. Now there's another group who'd benefit from some radical nip and tuck in the natural selection order of the species. Up until now Hawk was more than happy to let bird flu run amuck, let nature do her worst, it'd clear the earth of the whingeing hangers on, but when bird flu reached the fringes of the US of A, Hawk felt personally affronted by it. Stupid boss-eyed geese had landed on American soil, they'd invaded the land he loved; this was war. He rapped the table and heads turned his way.

'There are various problems associated with bird flu. I'd like to begin by prioritising.'

There were murmurs of approval from the flock around him, none of them had thought to take action until America waded in. They'd follow in his wake.

'From a few isolated outbreaks in the East, it's now spreading world-wide, globally there are pockets of infection. Its genetic make-up is shifting to become infectious to humans. The cases in the East particularly Thailand are well reported.'

The Thai ambassador looked sheepishly down at his papers, he had a sallow unhealthy glow to his skin, goose bumped as if he'd been plucked. He glanced up, avoiding eye contact with Hawk, 'we did everything we could, we burned millions of Chickens.'

Hawk ignored his mealy mouthing and moved on. 'We have no vaccine available for the vast numbers that may be affected.' Hawk wanted to get past this bit quickly. He'd been one of those strongly opposed to stockpiling vaccines, despite the whingeing and whining of bespectacled scientists, pulling their goatee beards bleating *It's not a case of if, it's a case of when.*

Hawk had prepared a report on their research and scoffed at their scare-mongering tactics; there was no need to panic. Hawk simply believed God would protect the just. The USA would be safe, all they needed to do was sit tight while the rest of the spongers and losers were wiped out. In the long run, the world would be a safer place.

'The final concern in connection with bird flu is that people are panicking, they are stockpiling food and the world economy is on hold. We all know money makes the world go round, and at this rate, we'll soon be at a standstill.'

The forum was opened up to discussion. They squawked and flapped round the table. There were flurries of activities as head bobbed and dived with ideas, the group was flustered with fear flitting and rattling across the nations, staccato voiced mouths opened and shut. A heavy-breasted German woman with very red lipstick declared shrilly, 'everyone should stay indoors.'

A lugubrious Italian flicked back his slick black hair and shook his head, 'we should watch and wait.' He lazily glided across the table for another cookie.

Two Oriental men chattered, high pitched, jabbing words, their heads waggling up and down. 'We should kill all infected.'

A beautiful Indian woman wrapped in swathes of rich indigo spoke gently, as if calling from a long way away. Hawk wasn't listening to words, he just heard their noises, the cawing and clacking, the clucking of fat hens at the end of the table, the Quack Quack of stupid small brains. He strained to hear the soft cooing of the Indian lady. He would've liked to have stroked her, feel the brightly coloured material, the flutter of heartbeat under her small breasts, to know the trembling of her tiny bones. At the same time, part of him would like to crush her pathetic body, wring her scrawny neck with a quick snap of his long trained hands. Hawk shook himself out of his daydream, he tapped his pencil gently on the shiny table, he liked to hear the knock of wood, it made him think of nights out in the wild woods with his father. Hunting and fishing by day, cooking meat round a crackling fire at night. It taught him to be a real man, to understand the animal world, survival of the fittest, the cruel rules of nature. As a child he shot birds without a bye or leave, without their wings flapping they were pathetically small and weak. Hawk felt the bird flu problem wasn't much different. Some viral wing clipping and the problem would be solved, he didn't want it eradicated, it was useful, bird flu could cleanse the world; Jesus Christ it was well overdue.

While they yakkity yakked, he glanced down at his arms. He flexed a muscle to see it jump and quiver under his skin. He was finely honed, a tuned specimen. He sniffed the nervous excitement round the table as their fears grew and they considered different scenarios *What if it's worse than the 1918 epidemic?...fifty million dead...How would we cope?...Dispose of the bodies?...The risk of infection?...Should we stop eating poultry?...Can we still wear feather hats?...How can we stop it?*

Their voices were rising to fever pitch, shrill warbling. Hawk contained a little smirk, they were so prone to panic, flying off on one tangent and then another. He approved of pecking order, natural selection. He let the smirk quiver on his lips; bird flu; bring it on.

Hawk was decisive and delivered the plan of action which had been hatched months ago by powerful men in grey suits. He was bored and needed some fresh air. He suggested some damage limitation was needed to stop the world spiralling into chaos. 'There will be no international or domestic flights until the crisis has blown over, or until an adequate stockpile of vaccine is produced. People will be advised to stay indoors. Schools and leisure facilities will be closed, public transport will be limited to bare essentials. Only a selected skeleton workforce will be operational. There will be curfews to ensure the majority of society stays indoors. It will be possible for police to make immediate arrests of those flouting the rules, and citizen arrests will also be feasible.'

'But it could be months before an adequate amount to protect the population is produced.' Screeched the Japanese minister.

He reminded Hawk of a cockatoo he'd once shot in New Guinea, the silence after the shot was screaming.

The group were still jabbering wildly. He was tired of their flights of fancy and closed the meeting, asking for the minutes to be circulated. He ignored their pleading doe eyes and shrugged, 'it's the only way to beat this Mother fucker.'

Hawk was above international flight embargo. His special status meant he could roam the skies freely. He soared from continent to continent, ensuring bird flu was contained, wishing it would escape to scourge the wayward lands that disgusted him. He grew restless. The weeks dragged, the advice for people to stay indoors seemed to be working, there were no more reports of bird flu. Families nested round their TV's, they nibbled nuts, foraged in their cupboards. They watched and waited, peering up out of their windows at scudding skies and billowing clouds. They watched the birds to see if they'd falter and fall. Two months passed and no further report of infection.

Hawk was fidgety and restless. He preened himself in front of the mirror. His eyes were lacklustre, his army medals looked tarnished, his black sleek hair, dull and lifeless. He was hungry for action, for the chase, the hunt, the kill. He received a message from medical research that day, 'Hawk, good news. We're on schedule to start the vaccination programme next week. It looks as if we've beaten this baby. God bless America.'

Hawk felt caged in. He was trapped in the weakness of humanity. He was glued to its frailty, the string of obligations to the useless no hopers who tugged and tethering him. Was he truly alone in realising bird flu was a Godsend, a necessary evolutionary step? Was everything going to be left to him? He slammed the door to his gym and did a furious workout. He pounded his body until he sweated and shook and felt in control, every cell in his body sharpened, he realised he knew what to do.

A private CIA jet was prepared for him immediately. He had some urgent work at the governmental research laboratories. He needed to discuss the genome for the 1918 virus. The vaccination programme was based on similar gene patterns to bird flu, the doctor in charge enthusiastically explained how they modified the virus to be effective against bird flu. 'We took the 1918 virus from a body frozen in Siberia, it's been hugely beneficial in the modification for vaccine against bird flu. Of course it's highly toxic in its own right, but it'll never escape this laboratory.' His bleep interrupted his interesting educational blurb; Hawk's secretary was very reliable.

'Excuse me a moment.' The doctor stepped aside taking the call, Hawk moved towards the test tubes and calmly popped the 1918 vial into his pocket replacing it with a replica he had with him. It had the correct serial code, and colour combination; only a select member of the intelligence service, Hawk included, was privy to such sensitive information. Hawk patted his pocket gently and handed the dud vial back to the doctor, who gingerly placed the vial of water back in the security safe. Hawk thanked the doctor for his reassurances and explanation, they shook hands. The doctor admiring, watched the tall straight back of Hawk leave the lab and muttered 'Thank God this country is in the hands of such an honourable fine man.' He saluted the figure leaving the building 'God bless America.'

Coughs and sneezes spread diseases. Hawk went to the toilet, broke the vial and snorted some liquid up, he blinked, his eyes watering, it was like chlorine from the baths as a kid. That evening he was speaker at a well publicised function to celebrate the diminished threat of bird flu, vaccinations were due to start on Friday. He coughed and spluttered into the microphone, 'must be allergic to crowds' he joked. Everyone who was anyone was there. They gave him a standing ovation, rapturous applause. He was the hero who had orchestrated their escape from mass death.

Hawk circulated the hall. He was patted on the back, his hand shaken. They compared him to the eagle on the American flag, protecting his country. Hawk could feel the virus battling with his body. He smiled, he knew he'd win, he'd prepared for this war. He felt his temperature rise, two hot circles of pride glowed on his face. He excused himself from the milling crowd of penguins and pink female flamingos, the fine plumage of high society, the peacocks in full array bowed letting him past.

He took the fire exit to the top of the high rise building, leaping steps two at a time. He needed cool air and breathed deeply, the breeze caressing the fire burning through him. The wind blew the hairs on the back of his sticky neck, ruffled his damp shirt. He stared out across the twinkling lights of the city, the blinking lives, all huddled round the TV praising him for saving their humble weak lives. Tomorrow they'd leave their homes, get immunised, be free of fear. They'll think they're safe. Hawk cackled with a little shiver. He coughed and sneezed and giggled while the 1918 virus flew free in the air. Millions of lives, and millions of spiny viruses would join together, and only the best would survive.

Hawk was ablaze, he'd liberated mankind, delivered it from a feeble future. He spun round and round, his arms outstretched, flying under stars. The sweat poured off him, he stripped his clothes off and felt light as a feather. He sniffed the night sky with his large hooked nose, his beady eyes scanning the milling millions below, beneath his being. The clouds rolled across a big fat full moon, the little people hugged themselves for the novelty of being free. Hawk caught the direction of the wind, he looked across the deep blue velvet horizon sequinned with stars, and with a lithe hop, skip and jump threw his head forward and launched into the night sky.

CINDERELLA

CHRIST, LOOK AT THE STATE! I MEAN DOES THE COMPANY GET a bonus for employing them?' To think our Cheryl applied for the job and was turned down.' 'I know and she's lovely your Cheryl, answers phone nice and always looks fab.'

'And look at her, the dog's dinner. Important innit first impressions and all that.'

Tania glanced over at Julie and Susan, they sniffed her smile away, they always did. Wearily she picked up her purse and went to the snack bar. Down the stairs she heard the clickity clack of Susan and Julie's shoes behind her. She glanced round, they'd linked arms laughing, ignoring her as usual.

Tania sat alone in the park feeding crusts to the ducks, the bread was old and stale. She'd been in her last year of law school when war broke out in her country. As an asylum seeker her qualifications weren't worth the paper they were written on, she'd landed this office job because she was quick and efficient; and cheap, very cheap.

The next day Susan sauntered up to Tania's desk and smiled, it was a quick slash across her face; gone too quickly, but at least she was making an effort.

'I'm having a flat warming party on Saturday, d'you want to come?' She waited tapping her foot, sucking a fingernail.

'I'd love to, thank you,' said Tania trying to make her accent sound less foreign.

'It's fancy dress, vicars and tarts. Y 'know what vicars and tarts look like don't you?'

Tania nodded and quickly took the bit of paper with the address.

'See you about eight, and don't forget to dress up.' Susan's scissor lips shut, and she was gone.

Tania folded and unfolded the paper all morning looking at the address. She'd make herself go. It was a chance to make friends and escape the aching loneliness of this city.

For the rest of the week she spent her spare time scouring charity shops. She picked up an itsy bitsy red sequinned dress, some fishnet tights and high heeled red shoes from Oxfam that were hardly worn. A thick circle of crimson lipstick and she was a smouldering tart. Camouflaged under her big coat she teetered to Susan's on her heels. She heard laughing and squeals as she tottered up the steps to the flat, she clutched the cheap bottle of wine she'd bought even tighter.

Susan answered the door in jeans and a blouse. She dragged Tania in confused into a crowded living room full of people respectfully dressed, not a tart or vicar in sight. Susan slipped behind Tania pulling her coat from her shoulders. There were gasps, titters, several splutters.

'Goodness Tania, you do look dressed up for a good night' Susan teased.

A man in a pink shirt snorted, 'you'll make a bob or two tonight I reckon.'

The room exploded in laughter.

Tania stuttered, 'but you said it was fancy dress?'

'Not me, must've been a communication problem, your English isn't as good as you reckon y'know.'

'That's right when you answer the phone we always have to pick up the pieces interpreting after,' Julie joined in, 'you make our job a lot harder than it should be.'

Tania stared at the wall of glaring faces, turned grabbing her coat and ran. She stumbled down the stairs, tripping on her stupid tarty shoes. Her heavy make-up ran smearing her face, heads turned as she fled the streets barefoot, hating every inch of this dump of a city.

Julie and Susan spent the next week giggling every time they saw Tania.

Tania worked alone, ate alone, slept alone. Loneliness filled her world.

At least I can make money she thought biting her lip, and concentrated on hitting targets, improving efficiency and doing as much overtime as possible.

Tania made her first friend working late at night. Bridget the cleaner leant on her broom chatting while Tania tip tapped her computer keys.

'I know all about being an outcast darlin'. The English are a shower of bastards.'

They spent nostalgic evenings reminiscing peat fires, Irish sausages, fiddle music, ham and cabbage. Bridget brought her in some soda bread. 'make sure you put a good dollop of butter on it, not marg.'

Harry the night watchman soon joined them. The three of them had comfortable evenings huddled round the soft blue, humming computer. Harry'd share his fruitcake and they'd do his crossword, explaining to Tania the strange foibles of the English language.

One night Bridget was telling Tania about St Patrick when the office door flew open. A tall dark stranger hovered in the doorway. Harry dropped his cake, and Bridget clutched her duster in a fluster. 'Why Mr Charles we haven't seen you in a long time.'

'Not long enough.' His voice deep, dark mahogany, 'nothing personal Bridget you know that. He waved, 'Hi Harry, who's your friend?' his eyes smouldered into Tania. She cursed herself for blushing.

Harry lifted a knowing eyebrow and introduced Tania. 'This is Tania she's new.'

Mr Charles smiled.

'Hi Tania' he said and dazzled a row of white teeth for Tania only.

'We thought you were travelling the world? 'If I'd known you were coming home I'd have baked you some potato cakes. Mr Charles loves my potato cakes'.

'I ran out of cash, Dad won't cough up anymore, says it's time to join the real world.' He shrugged, 'this is it.'

'So you'll be working here?'

'The old man insists. Don't know my arse from my elbow and I'm a company director apparently.'

'Ah sure Tania'll help you out, she's almost a lawyer and is virtually running the place.'

Mr Charles raised an eyebrow, 'hidden talents eh Tania?' He sauntered over to her desk and perched on the edge, 'could you teach me a thing or two?'

Harry and Bridget nudged and winked and bustled away in a puff of busyness.

Mr Charles sat close, 'shall we begin?'

Tania nodded seriously and showed him the company information that would be useful to him. She showed him stocks and shares, the employment profile and suggested ways they might increase efficiency, and give extra job satisfaction to the employees. He pulled up a chair to be near to her, their hair touched with a graze of feeling, he breathed deeply taking her in. A glance at his watch nudged her elbow, she crossed her legs and caught his shin, he smiled. Their eyes shone wide in the computer light, late and later talking in hushed voices, snatching glances, so close their skin burned.

Bridget and Harry peeped from behind a cabinet. 'It's written in the stars' sniffed Harry.

There was no hiding their love and lust, they were smitten. Each night Mr Charles would come down to the office for his lesson in the finer details of running a business, and each night their lessons ended in the open mouthed language of love. Harry and Bridget kept their secret, they brought them blankets and food, but the only thing that satisfied their hunger was each other. They made a pact to keep their relationship a secret. Mr Charles knew it would be difficult to have Tania accepted in the high society circles his father expected him to mingle in. They decided to bide their time, Tania was reluctant to spoil the magic with the likes of Susan and Julie jibing her.

During the day Mr Charles remained holed up in his higher kingdom. Soft carpets, percolated coffee in china cups, polished desks, gold cufflinks. He reclaimed his throne with an insight and understanding of the company workings that surprised his father pleasingly, while Tania stayed in her office corner, quietly smiling to herself.

'So what you going to wear to the Christmas party Julie?'

'Dunno if I can fit into my velour purple dress I'll wear that. What you going to wear?'

'Oh I've got this fab red halterneck, it looks gorgeous with my platforms. I hope I get a dance with Mr Charles, he's lush.'

'Not if I get there first, has he got a girlfriend?'

'No one seems to know. Rumour on the block is he's gay, he's oblivious to the flirt divert attention round here.'

'What a bloody waste. He's so dark and mysterious gives me shivers just thinking about him.'

'Well we're all in with a chance, because we don't know for definite he's gay, it's just gossip from the typing pool.'

'I'm going to look so gorgeous that even if he is gay I'll bend him straight.'

They laughed and looked over to Tania's corner, 'what you wearing Buggalugs? Maybe that tart's dress you wore to my party Ha Ha.'

Tania told Mr Charles about the gay rumour.

'Good, it'll keep the vultures off my back.' He played with a strand of her hair. 'Why don't you come? Let's just do it; who cares what anyone thinks, you're the one for me.'

'I think there will be easier ways to break the ice, particularly with your Father, and anyhow, I've nothing to wear. Really I'd rather not go, it'd be too difficult.'

'You look great in anything, but best in nothing.' He undid her dress buttons and she slipped out and into his arms.

Tania worked late the night of the Christmas party. Mr Charles had to attend, company etiquette. Harry and Bridget sat with Tania, Harry brought a tot of brandy and Bridget some Christmas cake but Tania still felt miserable.

'I think you should go, bugger what they'll say.'

'You don't know what the other girls are like, they'll make my life hell.'

'Don't let yerself be a second class citizen.'

'Bridget's right pet, come on, no arguing we'll get you sorted, pass me the phone Bridget,' he punched in a number, 'Hello Audrey love. 'Y'know that young lass I've been telling you about, well we're going to help her get to the Christmas do. Aye I know you said she ought to. She needs something special for it, okay I'll see you in five minutes.'

Five minutes later Harry's wife Audrey arrived; a blonde buxom no nonsense woman. 'Hello Pet, I've brought Mrs Patel with me, she's a wizard with her needle, isn't that right Mrs Patel.'

A small smiling Indian woman stood behind Audrey with armfuls of bright materials.

'We've brought lots of colours to try against you.'

'Mind you, you'll have your work cut out there Mrs Patel, there's not a pick on her, I've seen more fat on a greasy chip,' laughed Bridget.

Audrey played with Tania's hair, trying to tease it into a back-combed beehive. 'Take no notice Pet, there's nothing a bit of cotton wool padding can't sort out.'

The women scuttled Tania into the coffee room and danced round her, wrapping her in swathes of beautiful silks and satin. Mrs Patel's nimble fingers nipped and tucked, pinned and fastened. Tania emerged later magnificent in a glorious gown. Harry whistled, 'you look like a bleeding princess'

Bridget dabbed her eyes, 'Ah Jesus, Sure you're only gorgeous.'

Bridget's brother-in-law waited in his taxi outside. Tania stepped gracefully into his black cab and blew them all a kiss before being whisked away.

At the Grand Hotel she glided into the oak panelled hall. Mr Charles stood morose by the sweeping staircase surrounded by a gaggle of secretaries. False laughter tinkled off the chandeliers. Tania floated drawn towards him. Their eyes met across the crowded room. 'Excuse me.' He pushed through the powdered and perfumed hordes. He took Tania's hand gently with a bow, and placed his other hand in the small of her back, 'shall we dance?'

'Well who the hell's that?' sneered Julie.

'Dunno, but I'll make it my business to find out and make her life a misery.'

Tania and Mr Charles danced all night, no one else got a look in. They swirled and twirled and set the dancehall alight with grace and beauty. Neither took their eyes off the other.

Monday morning the office was awash with gossip. 'Who was that d'you reckon Julie?'

'Dunno, bloody skinny cretin, God I wish I could show him what it's like to have a real woman.' She wriggled her hips.

'That bloody golden frock, it was like one of those from a Paki shop.'

'Carol from sales says she's from Persia, some kind of royalty.'

'Is that Carol who swears she's a size twelve and wobbled round like a blancmange in a pink tutu?'

They laughed and kept an eye on all the office workers passing through from other floors looking for clues. Julie shouted over to Tania, 'Eh Buggalugs you work late, did you see anyone leaving in a golden frock Friday night?'

Tania shook her head and kept her eyes on the screen.

The secretaries were buzzing to find out who the mystery woman was. At coffee Carol was full of it. 'I'm telling you she had no shoes on. I reckon she's a bleedin' Hobbit, had horrible hairy feet, you must have noticed or were you all pissed as farts. He'll dump her like a ton of bricks once he gets a look at those hooves.'

Tania's face burnt. Shoes were the one thing Bridget and Harry couldn't sort, she'd kicked her own lace ups off going into the ball, the long dress covered her feet; or so she thought.

An hour or so later Steve the porter brought in Tania's brogues and dangled them in front of the office staff, 'someone left these at the dance, anyone know whose they are?'

Julie's eyes narrowed, 'ee, I recognise them from somewhere. It'll come to me, and if Carol's right they'll lead us to the golden slapper.'

Tania tucked her flip flopped feet under the desk, they were all she could afford, wondering how on earth could she get her brogues back.

The secretarial hubbub was interrupted by shouts from the director's office. There was a hush over the whole department as everyone tuned into the thunderous argument between Mr Charles senior and junior.

'I don't care about Miranda you want me to meet. I don't care if she has the right background, I don't care about her good city connections, and family ties in the right social circles. I've already told you I'm in love.'

'Oh for God's sake you let your imagination run away with you son.'

'No Dad listen to me, I don't want anyone else. I'm in love.'

'Well who is it?'

'We danced all night at the office party.'

'That skinny bint, good God, you can't be serious.'

'I'm sick of this facade, I'll show you how serious I am.'

Mr Charles junior stormed out of the office. He swept past the open-mouthed secretaries, past the admin. staff, past Steve the porter still dangling the shoes. He headed for the furthest corner of the office space where Tania's desk was tucked away. He gently rested his hands on her shoulders. 'Come on darling it's time.' Mr Charles pulled Tania up to her feet, he looked into her eyes, 'I can't spend the rest of my life living a lie, I can't pretend anymore.'

Tania stood close to him trembling, she reached out and put her arms on his waist to steady herself. He unbuttoned her cardigan and shrugged her out of it. He reached up and touched her face, fingers tracing round to her eyelids, peeling her false eyelashes off, he took a tissue and gently wiped her make-up away, smudging bruises on high cheekbones. Lastly he slid her bony shoulders out of her dress and as the office stood stock still in shock he slipped his fingers under Tania's boring brown bobbed hair and peeled off the wig. The costume of a woman lay redundant on the desk leaving a small male, dark haired Toni, sheepishly entwining fingers with Mr Charles.

Mr Charles unlaced the unclaimed brogues and knelt before Toni, slipping one foot in, then the other. He laced them gently and firmly, and looked up winking at his lover. They held hands and tip toed out, weaving through the boggle eyed gulps and gasps. They closed the door quietly behind them.

Bridget and Harry kept all the postcards they sent, looking up each country on the Atlas they'd pinned on the wall. They'd mull over the map while enjoying a bit of Bridget's home-made parkin. The affair caused quite a kerfuffle upstairs, Mr Charles senior sacked anyone on the spot found gossiping about it.

But in the empty office building at night Bridget and Harry were free to talk often about them, knowing love like theirs was a rare gift. 'Like a fairytale wasn't it Harry?'

'It was indeed Bridget, it was indeed.'

Idle Hands

TRUDI STARED OUT TO SEA SNIFFING SILENCE. 'THE TROUBLE is nothing ever happens. Early retirement seemed such a good idea, I didn't realise I'd be surrounded in decay so quickly; women with powdered mouldy skins, men, wrinkled and pruned. They smell close up, mothballs and peppermints, and something on the turn, like sour cream.'

'You don't smell yet Dear. Do you want a lolly?' asked her sister Joan.

'No thanks, I can't bear the thought of having to heave ourselves up again.'

'You need something to occupy yourself, maybe yoga. You have a beautiful house, a lovely garden, an agreeable husband, and two grown up children to be proud of. There's so much you can do now that you couldn't do when you were younger, and it doesn't have to be knitting or crochet. With just the small effort of a little smile and pink cardi everyone under forty will think of you as *sweet.* They'll offer their seats, shut windows for you in case you get a chill, and pack your bags at the supermarket to save them waiting 'til closing time. You can have sex without the worry of getting pregnant, and at your age, if you catch a sexually transmitted disease it's a coup, something to brag about at the over sixties swimming club. Eat, drink, and be merry. That's what it's all about.'

Trudi sighed and watched a frisbee hover across the sun. Joan read her Saga magazine for the next two hours while Trudi did nothing.

Joan sat up with a jolt, 'goodness me look at the time, Bertie starts panicking if I'm not back before sundown for our evening G&T.'

'You see the trouble is nothing ever happens,' whined Trudi.

Joan brushed herself down, 'Oh for goodness sake Trudi, go and get some HRT, you sound like an old record, going round and round.'

When Trudi got home she wandered through her tidy house and slumped on the cream settee. She threw her head back against the perfectly plumped cushions and shut her eyes, 'Oh God Larry'll be back from golf soon.' Larry annoyed Trudi; he loved being old. He liked his toupee, his dapper cravat, his loud checked trousers and the fact that he saw himself as "A bit of a character." Most of all he liked the ritual of old age, the All Bran of every day regularity.

Thinking depressed Trudi, she decided to make a cake, it'd been ages since she'd baked, and it might take her out of herself. She went through to the kitchen and switched the oven on, collecting ingredients, weighing and measuring. When it was ready to bake she realised the oven was still cold. Was anything in life straightforward? She dialled a local electrician who obligingly came soon, she left him to it while she watered the plants in the conservatory.

She hurried back when she heard the heavy thud. The electrician lay moribund on the tiles, white and unconscious. In a previous existence Trudi was a hospital Sister, she acted fast, rolled him over and thumped his chest hard. She had her lips hovering over his to give mouth to mouth resuscitation when he gave a weak groan. She helped him groggily sit up. The electrician sobbed, 'I nearly died, you saved my life.' He clutched her arm, 'I've had a near death experience.'

'There, there,' Trudi patted his back, 'you're fine now aren't you?

Perhaps we should've turned the electricity off first eh?'

'I saw the tunnel. Y' know the tunnel with a bright light at the end of it. Thank you. How can I ever thank you?'

Trudi helped him unsteadily re-gain his balance. 'You're fine, come on now, a cup of sweet tea and biscuits and you'll be ticketyboo.'

The electrician wiped his eyes, 'I could be dead.'

'But you're not, so finish your tea.'

The electrician nodded, did as he was told, wiped himself down, and stopped crying. 'Here keep the cheque,' he pushed it into Trudi's hand, 'don't forget if there's anything I can ever do for you.'

Trudi watched him go shakily down the garden path. As his van pulled away she span round, did a little dance and clapped her hands. She hadn't felt so good, or enjoyed something so much for years.

The euphoria didn't last long. A week later she was back in boring suburbia with nothing much to look forward to other than Bridge, flower arranging and good incontinence pads.

It was the Women's Institute meeting. Trudi didn't enjoy the WI, but it got her out of the house. She looked round the semi-circle of curled prawns wondering what are these old women to me? Marjorie the retired headmistress organised and delegated, 'Trudi if you and Gladys do the nearly new stall at the annual fair.'

Gladys tutted muttering, 'really, I would have thought Marg would have had more consideration, I mean old clothes could spark one of my allergies. I'd have been much better suited to the cake stall with Bernice, and Bernice and I are such good friends, we'd have been a good team.' She gave Trudi a look and sniffed.

The doors to the village Hall opened and shoals dabbled round tables; big-eyed, small-mouthed for a bargain. Gladys and Trudi stood behind their table of old clothes in silence until Gladys barked, 'Trudi you'll have to handle the garments, I'll handle the money. It looks like a load of shrunken dead sheep, it'll have me out in wheals and bumps, my skin's itching even looking at it.'

'That's fine dear, I quite understand.'

A stick-insect ginger-haired boy pulled out a stripy sock from the heap. 'How much for this Miss?'

'Five pence, and goodness me, what do you want with one long stripy sock?'

'It's to keep my caterpillar in.'

Trudi turned to Gladys to share a titter over the sock, but Gladys had gone to the cake stall for a chat with Bernice. Trudi spent the rest of the fair manning the stall alone. She heard the high pitched laughter of Gladys over at the soggy scone stall, and wished she'd been very rude to her.

The whole episode unsettled her, she needed distracting to calm down. She decided to make another cake, she'd give it to the Women's Institute, hoping the old bags choked on it. She thought about Gladys as she mixed and whisked, she was always looking for attention, with her allergies for this, and her allergies for that. The latest was kiwi. Trudi reached to the fruit bowl on a whim, chopped three kiwi's in stirring the mixture. 'There, a special Gladys cake.'

The following evening Larry answered the phone. 'Hello Bernice, no I haven't heard the news…'

Larry put the phone down quietly and turned to Trudi, 'Gladys is on Intensive Care Unit with a massive allergic reaction. They don't know what caused it, but she had to have an emergency tracheostomy because her throat swelled up so much she couldn't breathe.'

'Good Lord that's dreadful, Larry pour me a brandy.'

While Larry turned his back, Trudi punched the air, and kicked her heels, she downed it in one. He obligingly re-filled her glass, 'best thing for shock eh?'

Trudi didn't sleep well, she was buzzing, wide awake, and couldn't wait to get up and do something; anything. The image of Gladys on ITU made her giggle, she felt a thrill all over. The next morning she wasn't tired. In fact she had more energy than she'd had for years, even felt the old tingling yearn for sex. Larry munched over the Telegraph, Trudi nibbled grapefruit, tasted vile but was meant to be good for her. 'I think I'll visit Elsa.'

Larry put his paper down and peered over in his dreadful bifocals. 'Why? You said she depressed you last time. She can't have long to go now, probably won't be a pretty sight.'

'Well all the more reason to give some support.'

The staff nurse met Trudi and took her aside telling her quietly, 'Elsa's been moved to a side-room.'

Trudi understood the coded message, *not got long to go*.

So it was a bit of a shock to find her propped up in bed, looking in the rudest of rude health, except very thin, and certainly with all her faculties intact.

'Well don't look so horrified Trudi, what do you expect in the final stages of cancer.'

Trudi was expecting a weaker, less feisty Elsa. 'Em, so how are you feeling Elsa dear?'

'Super darling, as long as I have my little morphine pump by my side, I feel I could hang on for years. Oh don't look at me with such distaste Trudi, I might have to come back and haunt you. I'm quite happy y' know. I mean us oldies we're all going to die soon, so what if I beat you by a couple of years. I've said all my goodbyes, been told I'm much loved and will be missed, and all this attention, it's lovely. Anyhow enough about me, how's your lovely Larry?'

'Oh he's fine, sends his love.'

'Oh I bet he does, always had the hots for me did your Larry. All that bottom pinching and innuendo down the club at the nineteenth hole. Some men can't help themselves can they? And what about you? Still the perfect little wife? The only other man in your life is Mr Sheen. Gladys reckons it was all your cleaning muck that sparked her allergies off in the first place.'

Trudi jumped at the chance to be the first to tell Elsa about Gladys. 'Actually Gladys had a very bad allergic reaction recently. She's in a dreadful state, unrecognisable, swollen up like the Elephant man.' Trudi bit the side of her cheek to stop giggling. She prattled, 'now let me think, what other news have I… The Watsons won the couples' cup, and Frank Worthington won the club Trophy. The kids are fine. Katie has Ben at school and claims he's dyslexic, course we all know he's just stupid. Marjorie is stepping down as president of the WI to devote more time to her jams.' Elsa's eyes drooped sleepily, Trudi ploughed on, 'Larry's hoping he'll get on the board of the Conservative club, he's up against Arnold… Elsa, Elsa, have I bored you to sleep?'

Elsa snored, in sleepy abandonment. Trudi tip-toed to the little morphine pump chugging away. 'Gosh it's fascinating.' She stared at the mechanism and reached over giving the syringe a little shove. It moved along one of the notches. She pushed again, a little spurt this time, and the magic liquid squirted in. Elsa slept. She gave another little push, this time a whole five mls went smoothly sliding up Elsa's skinny arm. 'Oh dear, it's all gone.' Trudi looked at the syringe quizzically. She picked up her handbag, took a last look at Elsa sighing, 'Bye Elsa.'

When Trudi got home Larry was rummaging in the pantry. He grumpily shouted over his shoulder while foraging, 'you didn't leave me any lunch.' He turned round dropping the beans. 'My God what have you done to your hair?'

'I stopped at that new hair salon on the way home. A bit on impulse I suppose. D' you like it?'

'You look like one of those Greenham Common Lesbians.'

Trudi threw her handbag on the settee. 'Why don't you join the 21st century Larry?'

'Good God woman, have you gone mad? I'm going to the club for lunch. Don't wait up for me, I'll be late, very late.' He stomped to the back door slamming it behind him.

Trudi watched him 'pitiful' she sniffed. She picked up the phone and dialled 'Hello yes, is that Mr Burns the electrician? Yes, hello, I'm fine. Really you don't need to keep saying thank-you, although I have thought of a little favour you could do for me. Good, shall we say in a couple of hours? Great see you then, bye.'

Trudi twiddled a sharp tuft of newly sheared hair. She swung on her chair thinking *what a vexation Larry is, such a Killjoy.* She clicked her tongue, and settled herself on the Internet. The Internet was such a good idea. So many interesting bits and bobs you could pick up, all that up-to-date information at your fingertips. She typed in "Thallium poisoning" and smiled.

Larry was on his third scotch and soda, propping up the club bar with his pal George.

'So the thing is she seems to be losing her marbles. I mean with all this Alzheimer dementia around, it's a worry.'

George nodded as sympathetically as men's etiquette allowed. 'She's fond of her beef burgers too your Trudi, I mean it might not be a simple senile dementia, it could be that human form of spongioform BSE.'

Larry was a troubled man. 'She bought the Guardian this week too, I mean next it'll be joss sticks, Tofu and nut cutlets, she'll be saving whales instead of getting my lunch ready.'

George was getting a bit bored with all this women talk, 'I think she just needs to learn who's the boss again Larry. She's a decent old filly your Trudi, a few strong words'll sort her out, you'll see. Cheers.'

Trudi applied the last pat of blusher, and looked in the mirror well pleased as the door bell went. She ran downstairs in seductive negligee, high heels and lipstick, opening the front door in a flurry of heady perfume. 'Well hello Mr Burns' she purred, 'I've been waiting for you. Now about that little favour.' With no further ado, she led him upstairs.

When Larry arrived home hours later slightly pissed, there was a consolatory air. Trudi had washed her bright lipstick off, and flattened her hair into a more conservative style. She gently brushed his arm and pecked him on the cheek, 'I'm sorry darling, I've been behaving very badly recently. Old Age crisis eh?'

Larry was relieved 'well don't go all silly on me again. How about a nice cup of tea for your old man eh?'

'And I've baked you some biscuits to make up.' Trudi smiled.

The next day Larry felt rough, 'bowels are playing me up something rotten.' He burped loudly, looking slightly green.

Trudi hummed to herself as she popped on a cute pillar box hat, 'see you later'.

Larry wobbled unsteadily, 'Flu or something, my legs and hands are killing me, I feel bloody awful.' He spent his day from bathroom to bed.

The next day Trudi was attentive, spoon fed him home-made soup and tucked him up. When he drifted off she lay on the settee studying a take-away pizza menu. 'I feel like treating myself.' She ordered extra large, with garlic bread, some coca cola and a Mr Whippy ice-cream. She turned the TV up loud so she wasn't disturbed by his moans, and wiped the plates clean smacking her lips.

On Sunday morning Trudi went to church, 'I'll say a little prayer for you Larry and try and have some of the smoothie I made for you, it's full of goodness.'

She was flushed when she came in from the cold, unwrapping herself from her new bright scarf. 'They were all asking for you at church, I told them you'd soon be right as rain. They announced Elsa's funeral, I told them I didn't think you'd be quite up to it, but we'll see eh?'

Larry writhed, 'Oh God, I feel wretched.'

The next day Larry begged for the doctor, shivering under the covers. The doctor examined Larry rather curtly. A few sniffles fell off the pillow with a whisper 'Feel terrible.'

'It's flu, give him two paracetamol every four hours, the tremors are because of his high temperature.'

Trudi showed him out. 'Thank you doctor I'll make sure he has the flu jab next year, terrible man flu isn't it?'

Trudi went back upstairs, she plumped Larry's pillows, 'gracious, your hair's falling out. C'mon let's get this nourishing broth down you.'

That night Trudi slept in the spare room to avoid disturbing him, and to be honest he smelt rank. She tucked him in, 'I'll see you in the morning darling' and left humming loudly.

Trudi woke to the sun streaming through the curtains. She'd had a long blissful sleep and stretched in the warmth like a pampered cat. She eventually got up and tip toed into Larry giving a little start, 'good grief is that a cockroach? Lucky I bought that cockroach poison, and glad to see it really does work.' She looked at the bed for a few moments before turning and shutting the door behind her quietly. She hopped downstairs, did a couple of high kicks and a pirouette before sitting down and pinching herself. After a few moments of deep breathing exercises she reached for the phone, and dialled. 'Hello Joan, yes I'm sorry, I know it's early, but something's happened. Something's really happened.'